The
Iron Peacock

Also by Mary Stetson Clarke
PETTICOAT REBEL

The
Iron Peacock
Mary Stetson Clarke

Illustrated by Robert MacLean

Published by InquisiCorp Corporation, Littleton, CO 80122

First InquisiCorp Corporation Printing, 2005

ISBN 1-887840-67-2

InquisiCorp Corporation
8042 S. Grant Way
Littleton, CO 80122-2705
USA

To Edwin
my husband

Contents

1

Land Ho!

One bleak afternoon in early December of 1650, a young girl stood resolutely erect on the open deck of a ship scudding westward across the desolate gray wastes of the North Atlantic. Tense and dry-eyed, Joanna Sprague struggled for composure as four seamen bore toward the *Unity's* rail the broad plank on which rested the canvas-wrapped body of her father.

Clutching her blue-green velvet cloak about her, she lifted her chin above the prickle of its gold lace and turned her face so that the raw wind would not blow the hood's ribbons into her eyes. She had fought so hard to keep from weeping, she could not allow a bit of trimming to provoke a tear. She would not cry, she must not, although in all her sixteen years she had never felt so alone as she did now on this vessel, without family or friend or even another female aboard.

Before her were ranged the members of the *Unity's* crew. Every line of their bodies, every slant of their eyes, betrayed their indifference to the imminent burial. What cared they that one more soul had met death on the passage from England to the New World? It was a chance every voyager took. Lucky they were that the shipboard fever's virulence had not struck down some within their own ranks.

Beyond the seamen were massed the ship's passengers, if passengers they could be called. Scots they were, a hundred and a half, taken prisoner by Cromwell's army at the battle of Dunbar. Sold in London to the Company of Undertakers of the Iron Works in New England, they were being transported to Boston for resale as indentured servants. Disgracefully treated they were, more like cattle than men, her father had said, feeling some kinship with them through having lost his own family and home to Cromwell's soldiers.

For all the wretchedness of their imprisonment, the Scots stood stiffly erect, their richly colored plaids whipping against their gaunt bodies. She hardly dared look in their direction. Sympathy was the one thing she could not bear; it would unnerve her completely. She could sense the sorrow in their ranks. In the six weeks at sea many of the prisoners had come to know her father and to call him friend.

No more than a few seconds could have passed, but Joanna felt she had been standing here for hours, listening to the whistle of the wind in the rigging, the creak of hempen lines, and the swish of water against the hull. The footfalls of the bearers sounded loud in her ears.

With clenched jaw and rigid spine she waited. The four sailors passed in front of her. Would she ever forget the sight of their burden? They approached the rail, rested one end of the plank upon it, and hesitated, looking to the captain.

If only he would offer a prayer or say a few lines of scripture. But Augustine Walker was a staunch Puritan and opposed to any usage of the Church of England. Its burial service smacked of papism, he had told her, and was best omitted entirely.

Bits and fragments from her mother's funeral whirled in her mind like the faint, thin cries of the gulls circling high overhead. "I am the resurrection and the life. . . . The Lord gave, and the Lord hath taken away. . . . Unto God's gracious mercy and protection we commit you. . . ." How could anyone find heresy in such words of comfort?

Captain Walker said nothing, but lifted his hand in signal. The seamen raised the end of the heavy board. The canvas-sheathed form slid down it, then plummeted out of sight. A dull splash sounded.

For one unguarded moment Joanna almost dashed to the rail. But she stood her ground firmly. Even one surrender to impulse might shatter the composure she was fighting to maintain. Besides, she had no need to look. She could imagine only too well the weighted bundle sinking down, down, into the ocean's depths.

The sailors stepped back as if relieved to be rid of their burden. The captain turned to give an order, when from among the Scots massed on the other side of the ship came the wail of bagpipes. The eerie music rose with a savage keening of sorrow.

Startled, Joanna jerked her head about to scan the kilt-clad figures. In the rear ranks stood the piper, the young man her father had spoken of, scarcely older than herself, a tall, awkward youth with a shock of black hair. Ross

McCrae he was called. Kinsman to the Laird of Eildonan, he had been raised almost as if he were the laird's son. She'd watched him when the Scots had their daily airing, and had longed to ask his story. But she had kept her tongue still in obedience to her father's injunction to speak to no one on the ship. Beside the piper was a sandy-haired giant, squarely built, with an air of energy and high spirits. Her father had said he was Duncan Muir, as near a leader as the Scots had.

For a few minutes the music soared through the air, a burst of anguish, a torrent of grief. Then a roar erupted from the captain. His prominent brown eyes dilated, his florid face deepened in hue.

"Cease that racket! I'll have no heathen caterwauling aboard my vessel."

The music trailed away on a minor chord. In the near silence an emaciated Scot stepped forward, his gray hair and beard wispy in the wind. He must be Davison, the schoolmaster.

"'Tis a lament for the dead, sir," he protested. "In Scotland it is a custom—"

"There'll be no customs on my ship but those I make," thundered the master. "Get below, the lot of you."

A dozen seamen, taking their cue from the captain, began to herd the Scots toward the hold.

Joanna stood on tiptoe, straining for another glimpse of the piper. If only she could catch his eye, perhaps he would guess her gratitude. The lament was a fitting tribute to her father, and welcome to her ears, especially since nothing but her own prayers had solemnized his departure from this life.

Beside her the captain was speaking to the boatswain.

His voice had lowered to its usual gruff tone. "Send a man aloft," he ordered. "By the look of those gulls, land's not far off."

Joanna walked to the rail and looked to the western horizon. The waters of the Atlantic rose and fell in heavy waves, their tips feathered with spume. As far as she could see, the ship was no nearer land than it had been for weeks. Long weeks they had been, like an interminable, tossing bridge between her old life and the new one that lay before her, shadowy, mysterious, and unknown.

How cold the wind was! She pulled the cloak more snugly about her, grateful for the warmth of its fur lining. That was one thing she had found to be thankful for, when in the bleakness of her misery she had recalled her mother's oft-repeated admonition to count her blessings, then the woes would not seem so great. But how could anyone, least of all her gently reared mother, have imagined that tragedy and violence would have struck with such rapidity?

For a moment she could hear her grandmother's voice, as they prepared to leave for her mother's funeral. "Put this on, child. 'Twill be bitter cold in the chapel, and your mother would want you to wear her mantle."

They had left the gracious manor house, little dreaming it would be for the last time. Scarcely a quarter of an hour later, as the vicar was pronouncing, "The Lord lift up his countenance upon you and give you peace, both now and evermore," there had come the clatter of hoofs, the rattle of armor, and the shouts of a troop of horsemen. Her grandfather had given one glance out a window, then had pushed her and her father through the sacristy door at the rear of the chapel. She would never forget the sharp ring of the stained-glass windows as they splintered under the pikes of Cromwell's men. Somehow she and her father had managed to get mounts from the stable and ride off unperceived. Two days later, in London, word came that both grandparents were dead, the house and lands confiscated. Of the Sprague line, only her father and she survived, and they were being sought. That very night they had sailed on the *Unity*, without luggage or comforts or more money than had been in her father's pocket when they fled. To her people, as to a multitude of others, fidelity to the Royalist cause had brought death and desolation.

After the first seasickness, the voyage had not been so bad. She'd tried to be cheerful about having only the clothes on her back, she who'd been accustomed to rich attire. In the pocket of her mother's cloak she'd found a small silver-backed comb and a pocket handkerchief edged with lace. She made much of the find and daily combed her father's hair, mustache, and pointed beard when he became ill. The last thing she had done before the sailmaker entered the cabin with his roll of canvas and heavy thread had been to comb her father's shoulder-length, gently waving hair. It had once been golden brown like her own, but had grayed to the color of ashes. She had shrunk from touching his body after the life had gone out of it, but some sense of duty had demanded this last service of her.

If only her father could have been spared. If only he were standing beside her now, looking for a first glimpse of the New World. Would the prospect of the journey's end have lifted somewhat the cloud of grief and guilt that had engulfed him? To his dying day he had not forgiven himself for taking flight.

Dwelling on the past would do no good, she told herself sternly. She must look ahead. She must make some plan to find a means of livelihood in this New England. She had been taught to read and could write as fine a hand as any clerk. She could embroider almost as expertly as her mother, who had been noted for her exquisitely wrought handwork. Perhaps she might assist some lady of breeding who had set up a school for young girls. Or she might go into a nobleman's family and teach his daughters.

If both those prospects failed, she could work as a seamstress. Since early girlhood she'd watched her mother's gowns being fitted, and often when a seam or a dart was not right she had changed it herself, her mother being finicky, yet disliking to make many demands upon those who worked for her.

It was cold here by the rail. She shivered. But however chill and windswept the deck, it was better than the cramped gloom of the cabin, where the smell of sickness still clung.

Behind her a heavy step sounded. The scent of tobacco came to her nostrils. Captain Walker stood beside her, a pipe jutting from his mouth. He puffed judiciously for a moment, then removed the pipe and said, "Mistress Sprague, I regret disturbing you so soon after your father's death, but there are certain matters to be discussed, and little time in which to do it."

Though his voice was harsh, his expression was not unkindly. Joanna waited, feeling her jaw muscles tighten, her neck stiffen. She could not imagine what the captain wished to discuss.

"Know you aught of your father's pecuniary affairs?"

She shook her head. What a ridiculous question! Money had never been mentioned at home. There had always been ample, just as there had always been servants and stables and house guests and gaiety—though there had been neither guests nor entertaining since King Charles had been beheaded and the Puritans had come into power.

From his pocket the captain drew an account book and undid the brass clasp on the vellum cover. "When he came aboard the *Unity*, your father, like most redemptioners, paid only part of the cost of passage. He gave me fifteen pounds."

All the money he had with him the day they had fled for their lives, thought Joanna.

"The usual rate," continued the captain, "is five pounds per passenger from London to Boston, and five pounds each for food and drink. That makes a total of twenty pounds. So there is yet a sum of five pounds owing, which I must have, to turn over to the ship's owners."

Five pounds! It might as well be fifty, for she hadn't one solitary penny.

"What if a person dies, as my father did? Would not the debt be canceled?"

The captain pursed his lips. "The law says if a man gets halfway across the ocean, his passage must be paid in full. Now then, do you have the money, or don't you?"

"No," she said stonily.

"Do you have any relatives or friends in the Bay Colony who might pay the debt?"

Again she said, "No," then added, "My father hoped to

find friends of his younger days whom I knew not." It was true; he had not mentioned names to her.

"You're quite alone in the world?"

The words smote her with a dreadful finality, but she held her head erect. "Yes, quite alone."

The captain took a deep pull on his pipe. "In that case, then, there's only one thing to be done. Since you have no means with which to pay your father's debt—your debt now—you must work to pay it off."

"That's precisely what I intend to do," said Joanna proudly. "I mean to find work as a teacher or seamstress."

The captain regarded her keenly. "A laudable plan, but scarcely practical," he said. "I must have the money the day we arrive in Boston to give to the owners' agent. My only course is to turn you over as a bond servant to whomsoever will pay five pounds for your services."

Joanna stepped back incredulously. She couldn't have been more shocked if the captain had struck her across the face. A bond servant? She, Joanna Sprague? Bound to work as a menial for year after year until her term was up? She'd be little more than a slave! It was incredible; it was unbearable!

She could feel the telltale color flaming in her cheeks. "I'd as lief die!" she cried furiously, resentment hot in her blood.

Captain Walker regarded her coolly. "I feared you might take on in this way. Let me tell you that full a third of the newcomers to the Bay Colony are under bond to serve a number of years. Almost none remain servants, but find land and build homes of their own."

"*Servants own land?*" The idea was preposterous. No man of the serving class in England could aspire to be a property-owner. Only the nobility and gentry might hold title to land.

"On this side of the ocean land's cheap and ofttimes free," said the captain. "I've seen men rise from servant to freeman. I've known some to stand for town office. With women it's the same. A serving girl may marry a man of means." He waved an arm in a wide gesture. "You'll see it's far different here."

Different it might be, but she was not going to agree readily to going into service.

"Can you wait but a day after we reach Boston? Perchance I might find one of my father's friends there." Or perhaps she might find work and could persuade the captain to wait for payment.

"And take a chance on your running away? I've seen that happen too often." The captain's eyes held a cold glint. "You might as well make up your mind now to being indentured. At least then you'll be fed and lodged, and may learn a trade. If you're lucky, some man might even pay off your debt and take you to wife."

She could feel his eyes raking over her and shrank back within the cloak. No wonder he thought she'd need luck to catch a husband. Her skin was rough and dry from weeks of washing in salt water. Her hair, she knew, was stiff and greasy, darkened with dirt. Why wouldn't it be, after so long without soap and fresh water? Beneath the cloak her saffron satin gown was travel-stained and wrinkled. The damp got into everything. She must look, as she felt, completely disheveled. But that was no reason for the captain to cast this insult at her.

Someone might pay her debt and marry her? He might as well say some man would buy her as he would a horse or cow! Anything would be better than that—even being bound out as a servant.

"How long would I have to serve?" she asked, striving to keep her voice even. She couldn't let him know what the words cost her.

"Four years, maybe five, depending on who takes you." Was there a hint of relief in his tone?

Four years if she was lucky. She'd be twenty when her term was up. Surely by then she'd be able to take care of herself, even in a strange land.

"Very well, then, I agree," she said with as much dignity as she could muster.

"Agree!" The mockery in his voice stung her like a whip. "Can't you understand you've no choice? The picture has changed. The sooner you forget your old life and leave off your fine airs, the better 'twill be for you."

Forget her old life? Never. Its memories were all she had left. Leave off her fine airs? She couldn't fathom what he meant. Her parents had abhorred any affectation, had taught her to be civil and kindly to equals and servants alike.

The captain was turning away. "I'll see to the papers," he said, dismissal in his tone. She dipped him a curtsy and started toward her cabin, the need to be alone strong upon her.

Suddenly from high above, faint in the winter wind, came the long-awaited call. She strained her ears to make sure she had heard the words aright. Again they came, eerie and drawn out, with a rising note of triumph.

"La-a-and ho-o-o!"

Almost instantly the deck resounded with the rush of men's feet. The crew gathered at the rails. Scots peered from the open hatch. In a few seconds the captain had climbed to the poop deck and held a spyglass to his eye.

Joanna felt herself caught up in the moment's excitement. She gazed with intensity at the horizon. At first she could see nothing. Then, as the ship rose to the top of a swell, she made out a thin, dark line where the sea met the sky.

Despite her desperate situation, she felt a flicker of anticipation, almost of hope. Perhaps the future might not be so bleak as she imagined. There might even be some good in it.

2

Indentured

All the next day, as the *Unity* sailed shoreward, Joanna watched the town of Boston take on shape and color. From a mere line on the horizon, it became a jumble of steeply pitched frame houses pressed between the harbor and three hills, with wharves fringing the waterside and smoke rising from a forest of daubed chimneys.

The day following, the *Unity* was made fast to Long Wharf, a gangplank was put out, and the Scots lined up on deck for sale to the highest bidders. At the end of the row, next to the slight schoolmaster, John Davison, Joanna was ordered to take her place. For the first few minutes she was livid with self-consciousness. She was sure every eye on the wharf was upon her. But, as time passed, her nerves quieted and she could look about.

Long Wharf, like a road built over the water, was as busy as a market place, with longshoremen, carpenters, and apprentices hurrying about. Women with shawls over their heads hustled by, carrying a fresh piece of fish for dinner, or a head of cabbage. Children played in the street, jumping out of danger as horsemen rode past.

Overhead gulls soared, screeching raucously, darting down now and then to snatch up bits of refuse from the littered roadway. Shouts of workmen mingled with the cries of children, the neighs of horses, and the squealing of pigs that ran freely about, tripping the unwary. A strong odor of fish, salt, and tar blended with smoke from hundreds of hearths.

The first man to come aboard the *Unity* was young and elegantly dressed. He introduced himself to the captain as William Awbrey, factor for the Iron Works. He would select sixty-two of the prisoners for assignment to John Gifford, Iron Master at Hammersmith. He strode about, choosing this man and that, bidding them stand together in a designated space.

Joanna watched eagerly. She had located the young piper almost at once, hoping she'd have an opportunity today to thank him. But with others of the more sturdy prisoners he was early selected by Awbrey and moved to the opposite end of the ship from where she stood.

Soon the deck was filled with purchasers. They walked among the Scots, feeling their arms, examining their legs, even peering at their teeth, making loud comments the while. Good help was hard to come by in the Bay Colony, they said to one another. Workers got uppity and went off at the slightest excuse, or none at all. The only way to be sure of a man to work on a farm or in a shop was to get one bound by indenture.

Awbrey had collected perhaps thirty men when the captain accosted him angrily. Awbrey was not to take the best of the lot, protested the captain. The other buyers had a right to some choice. With a shrug of his shoulders, Awbrey told the skeleton-thin Davison to join the Hammersmith group.

Meanwhile the other buyers were busy. A sawmill-owner from Strawberry Bank took two Scots. A farmer from above the Piscataqua took another. From many parts of the Bay Colony settlers had come for servants, from Newtown, Newbury, Essex, Ipswich, and Marble Harbor.

A clerk using an upended hogshead as a desk filled out printed indenture forms, writing in the date and the names of master and servant. The forms were handled with great care. They were more than receipts for the sixteen pounds given for each Scot; they were legal, binding contracts, ensuring that, after seven years of service, the indentured man would be granted his freedom and given equipment to start a new life on his own. For most of them this meant a new suit of clothes, footgear, an ax, and a musket.

Captain Walker passed among the buyers, answering questions and giving instructions. Of one man after another he asked, "Have you need of a female bond servant? I've one here going for five pounds, a rare bargain."

Joanna could feel her cheeks burning as the men turned to look at her. When the first one approached, she wished she might turn to stone. But there was no escaping the scrutiny of his red-rimmed eyes. With obvious amusement he surveyed her blue-green velvet cloak with its bands of wide gold lace, her hood with its ribbon ties.

"She looks more like a pranked-up poppet than a scullery maid." He sniggered to his companion.

The other, lean and saturnine, with a twist to his thin lips, ran his eyes over her coolly. She fixed her gaze on a small cloud on the horizon and waited, hardly daring to breathe.

After interminable minutes he said, "She's too fancy for hard work. Thin, too."

"No meat on her bones," agreed the other. And they walked away.

Joanna had scarcely time to take a deep breath before another man approached. In a short time he too left, saying, "I need a strong wench that can lug buckets of water and firewood."

All day it was the same. No one seemed interested in taking her. And she could not have been more pleased. If no one would buy her time, she might yet be able to work off the debt in her own way, as seamstress or teacher. But Captain Walker was not a man to give up easily.

In the afternoon, when the last Scot had been spoken for, the captain took Joanna firmly by the elbow and hurried her across the gangplank. The Scots assigned to Hammersmith still stood in a group, waiting. As she went by, Ross McCrae lifted a hand as if in farewell. She turned her eyes toward him and tried to smile, but it was a sorry attempt. She'd had no chance to thank him, and now she probably never would. Soon he'd be on his way to Hammersmith, wherever that might be, and she—heaven only knew where she would be.

Across Long Wharf from the *Unity* was a warehouse with four women lined up in front and several men standing about.

"Do you stand over there with the rest of the females," ordered Captain Walker. "Folk looking for maidservants come to this spot. Someone is sure to bespeak you soon."

Two of the four were red-faced, buxom young women, gaily chaffing with the men. Barmaids both they were, and their master's widow hoped to sell their unexpired time to another tavern-keeper. A buck-toothed girl, lean and rangy, was there because her only relative, an uncle, could afford to keep her no longer.

The woman next to Joanna was a somber figure. Tall and slender, she had high cheekbones, copper skin, and hair black as a crow's wing. She must be an Indian, Joanna realized in excitement, trying not to stare. The woman stood with quiet dignity. She was clad in a dark gray cloak, the folds of which she extended to cover partially a young boy. With bright black eyes he peered out at the folk passing to and fro. When a pig, chased by an irate farmer, ran into and upset a sedate gentleman, the boy laughed, looking to his mother for an answering smile. But she regarded him with a steady, sorrowful gaze in which there was no spark of mirth.

Soon the barmaids went off with a beefy giant of a man. The rangy girl was taken away by a pinched-faced old woman and looked none too happy about her new mistress. Only Joanna and the Indians remained.

Beside Joanna, Captain Walker tapped his foot impatiently. Behind the Indian woman her squint-eyed master whistled nervously between stained, crooked teeth. The afternoon drew on.

A seafaring man approached, his gait rolling and his clothes redolent of oakum. A receding forehead, prominent nose, and narrow jaw gave him a ratlike appearance.

Joanna drew back instinctively, revulsion and fear sweeping over her. To her intense relief, the man glanced at her but briefly. Clearly he was interested in the Indian woman.

"What's this, a Pequot squaw?" he asked. "I've not seen one on the market in a long time." He spat onto the stained boards of the wharf.

The squint-eyed man stepped out eagerly from behind the Indians. "I got her in New London in the Pequot War. My share of the spoils, she was."

Joanna drew in her breath. She had heard of the Pequot War. Its savage cruelties, committed by red man and white, were known even in England.

"And the boy?" pursued the rat-faced seafarer.

"He's mine too, born in my barn six months after she was took prisoner. An extry dividend, ye might say." He laughed coarsely.

The sailor chewed reflectively, then spat again onto the dock. "I've no use for the boy. He'd eat more than he's worth. But I might take the woman off your hands. She could fetch a fair price in Cadiz."

The squaw's eyes burned fiercely. She clasped the child to her in fierce possession.

There were a few minutes of haggling. The seafaring man counted out heavy coins. The other produced a piece of paper, a pen, and a small pot of ink.

"What be ye called?" he inquired, pen poised.

"Abner Leach, always ready to pay a price for a red-skin." He pointed to a dingy vessel anchored a few rods beyond the *Unity*. "Yonder's my ship, the *Hydra*. And who might ye be?"

"Jeremiah Grubb." The squint-eyed man stuck out a leathery palm.

Leach extended stained fingers. The two shook hands.

When the bill of sale had been written and signed, Leach put a hand on the Indian woman's shoulder and gave her a shove.

"Come along, you," he said gruffly.

Still keeping the boy under her cloak, the squaw took a step after Leach.

"No, he stays with me." Grubb bent to take the child. The woman struck out at him furiously, the boy clinging to her. But her efforts were in vain. The two men separated mother and child, and Leach led the squaw away, struggling and protesting at every step.

Joanna found herself shaking. Helplessly she watched the squaw as she was forced to climb down the side of the wharf to a small boat and was rowed out to the *Hydra*. The Scots too were watching the Indian woman from the deck of the *Unity*, where they still were grouped, their tartans glowing in the late-afternoon sun.

The woman climbed a swaying rope ladder to the *Hydra*'s deck; Leach followed and hurried into his cabin, leaving her alone. For a few minutes she stood beside the rail in tragic desolation. Then she gave a piercing scream. Her figure hurtled downward from the ship, struck the water, and disappeared.

Captain Leach dashed out of his cabin, shouting orders to his crew. Three sailors hurriedly descended the ladder to the rowboat.

At the same time there was swift movement on the *Unity*'s deck. Ross McCrae broke away from the other Scots and ran to the rail. He had thrown off his cumbersome plaid and was poised to dive when Duncan Muir caught him in a strong grip. His voice was clear and urgent.

"Dinna be daft, lad. Ye canna reach her in time. Besides, ye'd be doing her nae service. 'Tis her wish to die."

Joanna strained her eyes for a glimpse of the Indian woman. There was no sign of the dark head—only the waves sparkling in the sunlight, and the gulls swooping and crying. And, by the rail of the *Hydra,* Captain Leach brandishing his fist in anger while his men rowed futilely about the area into which the woman had plunged.

The boy! Too late Joanna thought of him and bent toward him. By the terror on his face, she knew he had seen all that had happened. She opened her cloak to take him under it as his mother had done, but he edged away from her to stand in solitary hostility.

Grubb exhibited no discomfiture whatsoever at the woman's suicide. With obvious satisfaction he weighed the coins in his hand. Joanna could almost hear him saying it was a good thing he'd got his money before the squaw ended her life.

A few minutes passed. Then a kindly-faced man, slight and stooped, drew near. Was he looking for a maidservant? He'd make a fair master, she felt. Perhaps he was the one she was destined to serve.

The newcomer, however, peered past her to look at the boy.

"I want a lad small enough to walk under my looms and tie the heddles and broken threads," he said to Grubb. "This one might do. What's his price?"

"Four pounds."

"Too high. I can get a white boy for that." He turned away.

"Make it three, then," conceded Grubb.

"All right. You have the papers?"

Again money changed hands. The pen scratched, and the thin man led the boy away. Though his small face was screwed up in woe, not a tear streaked his cheeks. Pulling his hand out of his new master's, he walked beside him, stiffly erect. Joanna could not help admiring his pathetic courage. She hoped the man would be as kind as he appeared.

How much longer she stood there beside Captain Walker she hardly knew. She kept hearing over and over again the Indian woman's scream. She could almost feel the icy waters closing over her own head. She would never forget the woman's tragic dusky face, nor that of the child.

She was startled from her thoughts by the approach of the elegant Mr. Awbrey. With him was a red-faced young man clad in the loose breeches and leather jerkin of a workman.

Mr. Awbrey waved his broad-brimmed hat in a wide arc as he bowed to the captain, and announced ceremoniously, "This is one of the Iron Works boatmen. He's come from Hammersmith to fetch the Scots and brought me a message from John Gifford. Found me in the tavern, he did."

Mr. Awbrey had been in the tavern most of the afternoon, judging by the aura of rum about his person.

"The Giffords desire me to find them a kitchenmaid and send her to Hammersmith with the Scots. 'Tis too late in the day to look elsewhere. This comely damsel is the one I'll send to them." He chucked Joanna under the chin, bending toward her with a toothy smile. She shrank back beside Captain Walker.

"Have you the five pounds?"

"That I have." Awbrey slapped the captain on the shoulder.

"Very well. Come along to my cabin and we'll make out the papers." His relief at disposing of her rang loud in every syllable.

In a few minutes they were back on the *Unity,* in the captain's cabin. He drew from his desk a printed indenture form and filled in the date, then paused before a space for the master's name.

"Shall I make this out to John Gifford, with you signing as his agent?" he asked Awbrey.

"Yes," Awbrey assented.

The captain's pen scratched busily. From where she stood, Joanna could look over his shoulder and read the printed words.

"This indenture made the 8th day of December in the year of our Lord 1650 between Joanna Sprague and John Gifford, Iron Master, witnesseth that the said Joanna Sprague doth hereby covenant, promise, and grant to and with the said John Gifford during the term of four years to serve in such employment as he shall assign. The said master well and faithfully she shall serve, his secrets keep, his commandments lawful and honest gladly shall do." There followed a list of restrictions. She was not to waste her master's goods, nor lend them, nor to play at cards or dice. The Iron Master was to provide meat, drink, clothing, lodging, and all other necessaries according to the custom of the land. "In consideration whereof the said John Gifford shall pay unto Augustine Walker the sum of five pounds."

Across the middle of the sheet ran a row of punctured dots, or indentations, by reason of which the document was termed an indenture. Below was printed a duplicate of the contract. This too Captain Walker filled in painstakingly with the date, names of servant and master, and the term of service.

At the bottom of each portion were spaces for signatures, beneath the words, "In witness whereof the parties abovementioned to this indenture have interchangeably set their hands and seals."

Captain Walker handed the paper to Awbrey. He took the pen with an unsteady hand and signed his name, adding beside it, "for John Gifford." On the other half of the contract he signed again.

The captain then affixed his signature with a flourish in both spaces and gave the pen to Joanna.

Reluctantly she took it in her fingers, slowly dipped it in the ink. If only a thunderbolt from heaven would strike the pen from her hand and consume the document in a burst of flame.

"What's the matter?" asked the captain. "Don't you know how to sign your name?"

She threw him a searing glance. Did he think she lacked education as well as money? She'd show him she could write. Swiftly she inscribed her name, first on the top half, then on the bottom section.

Awbrey stooped over her, peering at her signature. "You write a pretty hand," he said. She glared at him.

The captain shook sand over the wet ink, let it dry a few moments, then blew it off. He folded the paper across at the dots, then tore the halves apart.

As in a trance, Joanna accepted her portion, folded it, and put it in her pocket. The crackle of the paper sounded as sinister as a death knell. Pretty hand or not, she had just signed away four years of her life. Four whole years.

The captain waved her to the door. "You can go to your cabin now. Tomorrow at dawn you'll sail with the Scots for Hammersmith."

Woodenly Joanna dipped a curtsy and made her exit. The deed was done. She'd signed herself away. Yet even in this desolation was one faint glimmer. She would be near the Scots. They had been her father's friends. Perchance they would be hers.

3

Up the Saugus River

By noon of the following day, the two shallops belonging to the Iron Works had left Boston Harbor far behind and were well on their way northward along the coast. The vessels pitched and tossed as they cut through the choppy sea. Besides a crew of three, each carried about half of the sixty-two Scots bound for seven years' service at Hammersmith Village in Lynn.

To the east the heaving waters of the north Atlantic rose white-capped against the sky. On the west stretched the bleak Massachusetts shore, its sandy beaches and ice-coated ledges lashed by waves. Inland an occasional cleared field and wisp of smoke gave hint of human habitation in the seemingly endless forest.

Joanna huddled in the lee of the first shallop's after bulkhead, grateful for its scant protection. Even here the wind tore at her hood, blowing locks of hair about her face, stinging her cheeks. It tugged at her cloak, striking through the fur lining to her very bones. How much more keenly it must cut through the Scots' threadbare plaids. Out here in the open boat, with the wind flinging their tattered garments about their emaciated bodies, tangling their unkempt hair and beards, they seemed more like scarecrows than the remnants of the force that had marched against Cromwell three months before. She had been told of the battle by her father, who had heard of it firsthand from the Scots.

It seemed incredible that so short a time ago these men had advanced, stalwart and courageous, colors flying and kilts swinging to the stirring skirl of the bagpipes. Now they sat silent and dispirited for the most part, shoulders hunched against the wind, each apparently lost in his own thoughts.

Just ahead of Joanna was Duncan Muir, as quiet as the others, his usual high spirits stilled, his eyes inward-looking. On her left, sharing the bulkhead's protection, John Davison sat, his head resting on his bent knees. He had swayed as he came aboard the shallop in the morning's first light. Since then he had dozed, wavering between sleep and wakefulness. Her father had shown exactly the same symptoms when he had first come down with the shipboard fever. And he, though younger and stronger than Davison, had succumbed. What chance, then, had the Scot in his weakened condition? She wished she could lay her hand on his forehead to tell if it was hot, but he had pulled his plaid up over his head and looked more like a bundle of rags than a man.

Close by stood the steersman, feet planted wide apart on the rough planks. With one heavy hand firm on the tiller, he kept his gaze on the sails and the sea ahead, save for an occasional glance at Ross, who crouched on his right, eagerly plying him with questions.

"Ye say the Iron Works are on the Saugus River. How much farther must we sail ere we reach the stream?" Ross was scanning the coastline, one hand shading his eyes.

"See that long spit of sand up ahead with two bits of land at the end, summat like islands? That be Nahant. Just this side of it is Lynn, and the Saugus River." The steersman pointed with a reddened hand.

"How far up the Saugus is Hammersmith?" asked Ross.

"Not far. We'll get there ere nightfall if the wind holds."

Joanna glanced astern. Behind them the second shallop followed steadily. The steersman squinted at the sun high overhead.

"Break out the bread and water," he bawled to the two crewmen.

Bread and water. More weevily ship's biscuit, Joanna supposed, like the *Unity's* usual sorry fare.

To her amazement she was handed a quarter of a crusty brown loaf. Its very fragrance was tantalizing. She bit off a chunk, chewed it voraciously. How utterly delicious it was! She'd nearly forgotten what fresh bread tasted like. This was made of rye flour and a coarser grain. It was chewy, with a nutty flavor. She couldn't remember when she'd relished food quite so much.

Next came a gourd of water, dipped from a hogshead amidships. The first mouthful tasted better than any drink she'd ever known, sweet and refreshing. The stuff aboard ship had been so stale and foul she'd had to pinch her nostrils before taking a sip.

Around her the Scots were tearing off mouthfuls of the

crusty bread, wolfing them down. Even Davison had poked his head out from his tartan wrapping and was munching a bit of crust. He quaffed deeply of the water.

"There's naught can match pure water for quenching a man's thirst," he said, wiping his mouth with the back of his hand. His face was flushed, and his eyes were bright.

"How do you feel?" asked Joanna anxiously.

"A bit light in the head. But dinna fash yerself o'er me, lass."

Joanna laid her fingers on his forehead. As she suspected, it was burning.

Davison gave her a weak smile and let his head droop forward to his knees again. " 'Tis that giddy I am," he said apologetically.

If she could make a place for him to lie down, he might be more comfortable. She lifted her head and spoke to the steersman. "Have you something to make a pallet of?" she asked.

"We've a sail, mistress, and some old sacks. Would they do?"

In a few minutes she had folded the canvas into the semblance of a bed, placing it close to the bulkhead for shelter in the spot she had occupied. Davison stretched out gratefully.

In her new exposed position the wind cut at her sharply. Almost before she could feel its full force, Ross held out a strong arm toward her.

"If ye'll step over to this side, ye may find a bit less of a draft."

A draft! She couldn't help but laugh. It was more of a gale, to her mind.

He steadied her as she stepped around the helmsman,

then laid one of the sacks over the rough planking for her to sit on. It had been so long since anyone had done anything for her, she couldn't have been more pleased if he had set out a satin cushion. He seated himself a little distance away from her, his body shielding her somewhat from the chill gusts.

" 'Twas good of ye to take care of Davison," he said. "Is he verra ill, do ye ken?"

"I fear he may be, but I know little of sickness. Only what I saw when my father—" She faltered. Why did her voice have to break that way?

" 'Tis verra difficult to bear such a loss. I ken well how ye feel." His voice held a note of sorrow that echoed hers.

For a moment she could almost forget her own grief. "Your father, is he—" She couldn't say the word. It was too harsh.

He guessed her thought. "Aye, killed at Dunbar. Had I not stopped to give him a decent burial I might not be here now. But I couldna have savored my freedom, thinking of him lying there a prey to beasts."

"You mean you could have got away, but stayed to bury him instead?" The agony of making such a decision!

"Aye. He would have done the same for me." The statement was matter-of-fact.

" 'Twas vastly loyal," she breathed. For a few moments they sat in silence. "I've been wishing for a chance to thank you," she continued, "for playing the lament for the dead that day. My father would have been pleased, I know. And I was most grateful." Why was she having so hard a struggle to keep back the tears, now that it was all over? She'd had far more control over herself on the day itself.

"I'd scarce begun," he said bitterly. "But if it gave you some comfort, I'm satisfied." He too seemed to be having difficulty with his voice.

Surely she wasn't going to cry. Not now. She blinked and concentrated on the skyline. But it was a blur of varying blues. She stole a glance at Ross. His face too was sad. "I fear I am but poor company," she said apologetically.

He looked at her grimly. " 'Tis not just you—'tis the whole boatload of us," he said. "There's nary a bright eye in the lot. A fine bunch of feckless gowks we be. Could we but catch a bit of our auld spirit!"

An idea struck her. "Could you play them a tune on your bagpipes?" she asked. "Something bright and cheerful?"

He shook his head somberly. "Nay. A gloomy piper canna play a merry note. 'Tis a well-known fact."

For the life of her she could suggest nothing else to court cheer. She sat quietly, hardly hearing the creak of lines, the swish of water, and the call of the gulls. The others too were silent, each intent upon his own concerns. She found her thoughts rushing ahead, flying on swift wing to the village of Hammersmith.

Life would be different there, she knew, not only in her own position of servitude but in the village itself. The Bay Colony had been settled by Puritans, and doubtless every soul living in it was rigid in adherence to Puritan beliefs, merciless in the pursuit of what he thought was right in the eyes of the Lord. She herself had known no Puritans, all her family's friends being Royalists. Would she be able to conform to the customs of this new land?

And Mr. John Gifford—what would he be like, this man she was bound to serve? The Iron Master: the words had a sinister sound. She envisioned a behemoth of a man, beetle-browed, tight-mouthed, with a stance as stiff as his stern mien and a heart as hard and unyielding as iron itself. She began to shiver from more than the chill wind.

Soon a shout broke from the steersman. "Yonder's the Saugus River. Look sharp. We're coming about."

Riding low in the choppy sea, her crowded deck only a few hands' span above the billows, the vessel turned westward toward the river's mouth. A wave hit broadside, throwing a sheet of water over the gunwale, striking Davison as he lay on his pallet. He roused, gasping, as the icy brine struck. Wisps of thin gray hair lay wet upon his hollow cheeks. Coughing, he raised a hand to brush away the drops.

Joanna made her way to his side, put a hand on his plaid to draw it about his shoulders. Ugh, the cloth was soaking wet. Davison was shivering, though his head seemed hotter than before.

Joanna sat back on her heels, wondering what to do. Were there more sacks? Or another sail, perhaps? Suddenly she saw Ross bend down, unwind Davison's plaid from about his body, and replace it with his own, tucking the dry length of tartan carefully about the ill man.

Davison made a murmur of protest. "Nay, Ross, ye maun keep it for yersel'."

The other Scots looked at Ross in amazement. Joanna could almost read their thoughts. He was a good lad to give up his dry covering, but how would he keep from freezing in this bitter cold? They looked bleakly at him, then away. The helmsman stared open-mouthed. Ross alone seemed unconcerned. He stood calmly as sharp gusts beat against his grimy shirt and doublet, whipped at his kilt.

Duncan Muir half rose, asking, "Be ye not cauld, lad?"

"Cauld? Ye're daft, man. 'Tis but a bonny warm breeze," retorted Ross, laughing. A few minutes longer he stood there, a broad grin upon his face, while his skin turned purple. Then, with a swift movement, he dove to the deck beside Duncan Muir.

"Share yer plaid wi' me, Duncan, or I'll wrestle ye for it."

Duncan threw out a hairy arm, holding open one end of his plaid. "Come to yer mither, then, me wee bairn." His blue eyes crinkled beneath his sandy thatch. "A bit of a brawl would warm us, at that, were there room for it," he allowed.

A guffaw arose from the men. Joanna could not help joining in the laughter. Even Davison managed a feeble smile as the two struggled in mock contest for the wool covering.

The river had begun to narrow and the wind to slacken, though the shallop still drove steadily through the water. The marshes that lined the river's mouth gave way to wooded slopes, where among the trees' bare branches bluejays screamed and squirrels chattered. Scallops of ice bordered reeds and grasses at the water's edge. Now and again appeared a dwelling, little more than a roof and broad chimney visible from the river. A whiff of wood smoke and of something more—could it be fresh meat roasting on a spit?—tingled Joanna's nostrils.

Duncan Muir's voice rose. "Can ye tell us something of the Iron Works?" he asked the steersman. "Is it true that it's called one of the wonders of the New World?"

" 'Tis the greatest wonder, to my mind," came the reply. "Folk come from all over the colony to look at the furnace and forge. Even the Indians travel a great way to look at it. They think Mr. Gifford has some magic power for the making of iron." The steersman warmed to his subject, encouraged by the rapt faces of his passengers.

"Wait till ye see the furnace in full blast on a dark night. 'Tis a fearsome sight. And when all the water wheels are turning and swishing, and the hammer is making a thunderous racket, ye'll think ye've never seen the like."

Joanna listened, her mind fastening on each detail. What would the Iron Works be like? She had no more idea of their appearance than she had of the other side of the moon. She looked at Ross. His face was intent, his gaze eager, as he stared ahead.

"Hark! Ye can hear the roar now." The helmsman held up a beefy hand.

Silence settled on the shallop. The soft burr of the Scots' voices ceased. Davison cupped bony fingers to his ear.

Then she heard it, a deep heavy sound beneath the caw of crows, the shrill of jays, and the slapping of water against the bow. As the shallop progressed up the river's winding course, the sound grew to a distant rumble broken by repeated thuds. Joanna could feel her senses quivering as the noise grew to a mighty thunder.

The boat rounded a bend in the river, and suddenly, dramatically, there were the Iron Works, with chimneys belching forth smoke and sparks, massive wheels turning in swift spray, and workmen hurrying in and out of cavernous structures from which shone a red glow.

Beside her Ross let out his breath in a long sigh. "A man couldna wish to see a grander sight," he breathed, his eyes wide with wonder.

4

The Iron Master's House

The shallop drew neatly alongside a small wharf, and Joanna looked up at a hillside fanning out like a vast amphitheater. Part way up its slope were the three main structures of the Iron Works. At the crest of the hill stood a stately dwelling, and beyond it other houses and a string of cottages.

While she gazed in amazement, people began to stream down the hill. First came two small boys, muffled in caps and scarves, their cheeks and noses cherry-red. Then women appeared, picking their way carefully down the frozen hillside. They wore short cloaks or soft-hued shawls thrown over their heads and crossed over their bosoms. Below their full woolen skirts showed sturdy leather shoes. Soon they were joined by men in leather trousers and aprons, some wearing rough jackets, others heavy shirts and jerkins.

On the fringe of the crowd two girls tugged at the hands of an older one. The two were very fair, with long blond hair streaming over blue mantles, their china-blue eyes round in pink-and-white faces. The older girl was as dark in coloring as they were light. Her skin was copper-brown, her black hair hung in plaits, and about her forehead she wore a band of intricate design that glinted in the sunlight. Her crimson cloak, her dark green skirt, were no different from the other women's, yet she stood out in the crowd like a tawny lily in a garden of English primroses. While every other eye regarded the newcomers with unfeigned curiosity, she kept hers averted and tried to draw the girls away from the gaping crowd. Joanna could see the hostile glances women threw over their shoulders at the Indian girl. More plainly than words their lifted chins indicated their dislike.

At the top of the hill a man appeared, fair-haired and slight. He walked swiftly toward the wharf, his dark blue cloak parting to reveal a rich gray doublet and knee breeches. He nodded as he passed through the crowd, with a word to one and another. Women bobbed curtsies; men touched their forelocks.

The steersman jumped to the dock. "Here be your prisoners, Mr. Gifford." He bowed his head deferentially.

Joanna sat open-mouthed. Surely she had heard aright. This must be the Iron Master, this handsome, well-favored man. A little of her dread dissolved. Perhaps she had painted the future too black.

Stumbling to her feet, she smoothed the folds of her cloak, wrinkled from the damp planking. Looking up, she saw the Iron Master's eyes upon her, his gaze questioning.

"And whom have we here?" he inquired, taking note of her shimmering blue-green velvet and glittering gold lace.

"Your new bond servant, s-sir," stammered the steersman, his once booming voice far from confident.

"My servant—*this*? From her bright plumage I took her rather for a peacock!"

The crowd took up the word. Joanna heard it echoing and re-echoing. "Peacock . . . peacock . . . peacock." Had she not been so vexed she could have wept. She, likened to a peacock, when she was feeling more like a bedraggled sparrow?

Beside her, Ross took a swift step forward, his black brows drawn in a frown.

The steersman found his voice. "She's not what you think, sir," he said earnestly, "but the daughter of a redemptioner that died on the way over."

"Oh?" Mr. Gifford's voice rose questioningly. "Could you not get one better suited to kitchen work?"

"By the time I found Mr. Awbrey, she was the only one left," said the steersman.

"Very well," said Mr. Gifford shortly. He looked past Joanna to Davison on his pallet. Again he turned angrily toward the boatman. "I specifically stated that the men assigned to me must be well and sound and free from wounds. What ails this fellow?"

The steersman's ruddy face had turned a darker hue. "He was able to walk aboard, sir, but took sick on the way."

Davison struggled up and leaned against the bulkhead. " 'Tis but a passing weakness."

"It had better pass quickly," warned Mr. Gifford. He turned and surveyed the others. "Get them ashore," he told the boatman. "I'll see to the other vessel." As if in afterthought, he added, "And take the girl to my house."

In a daze Joanna stepped from the shallop to the dock. She could feel every eye riveted upon her, taking in each detail of her appearance, from the ribbons on her hood to the silver buckles on her damson leather shoes. Beside her walked Ross and Duncan, supporting Davison. Ross kept turning his head to stare at the Iron Works.

The surging crowd, satisfied that the second shallop held no special excitement, straggled up the slope. The show was over for today, and they were eager to get back to the warmth of their homes. Though she scanned the strange faces, Joanna saw no more of the two small girls and their Indian companion.

At the crest of the hill, the boatman turned the Scots over to a clerk who began to write down the men's names, one by one. Then he approached Joanna. "Come this way."

The late afternoon rays of the sun had thinned. Suddenly the world seemed very bleak. Had she the courage to leave the Scots, her only link with her father and her former world? She looked at Duncan and Ross, who held Davison erect with difficulty. "Good-by," she said softly to the three, then turned to follow the boatman.

Before she had taken a step, a voice sounded in her ear, a young voice with a Highland burr. "Courage, lass," it said. She did not need to turn to know that Ross was the one who spoke. The words cheered her immeasurably. She squared her shoulders and braced herself for the next encounter.

The Iron Master's house was an imposing structure, three stories high, with gables and mullioned panes. The boatman led her past the heavy iron-studded oak front door to the back of the house. At a plain wooden door he knocked. From within a muffled voice called out, "Ye can't come in now. I'm scrubbing the floor."

The boatman tugged at his curly forelock, puzzled. Again he knocked, shouting, "I've a message for Mistress Gifford."

"Go to the front of the house," said the voice crossly.

The boatman shrugged his shoulders, then led the way to the front door again and lifted the heavy iron knocker. After a few moments the door opened. A tall dark-haired woman peered out, then swung the door wide. Her lips parted in a smile more polite than warm.

"Pray come in," she invited, adding, "It is not my wont to answer the door myself, but my servant is otherwise engaged at present."

She waved Joanna inside, studying her closely, and continued. "Are you perchance the niece of the governor? 'Twas rumored she might travel with him this fortnight."

Joanna could see the boatman's face as the heavy door swung shut. The dismay written upon it would have been comical in any other situation. The trouble was, she herself was equally dismayed. How could she tell Mistress Gifford of her true identity without causing her embarrassment and arousing her antagonism?

She was about to say something to end the farce when the door opened abruptly, and the Iron Master strode in. At the sight of the two, he stopped short.

"Well," he asked his wife, "what do you think of your new bondmaid?"

"Bondmaid?" repeated Mistress Gifford. She lifted a ringed hand to her bosom. "Surely you must be jesting."

"Would that I were. We've need of a stouter wench than

this creature. Let us hope she'll be more useful than she looks."

Mistress Gifford's face had mottled. She turned angrily on her husband. "You might have given me some warning," she said. "For a minute I thought—" She bit off her words in confusion.

But she was too late. Her husband caught her meaning. "You thought she was some fine visitor!" He gave a mocking laugh.

Joanna stood silent between the two, infuriated as much by their attitude as by their words. They were behaving as if she were devoid of any feeling. Did they think she enjoyed her position?

Mistress Gifford led the way through a hallway into a large room on the right with crimson curtains at casement windows and carved chests hugging the walls.

On the broad hearth a fire blazed, lighting up two faces at the far end. An elderly woman in black gown and white cap sat stiffly in a wainscot chair. Beside her a child with a cloud of brown curls played with a wooden doll. She was a gay little figure, with green stockings showing below a scarlet gown and lace-trimmed pinafore. At the sight of Joanna she rose and made a curtsy, her face dimpling in welcome.

"No, Deborah, you must not curtsy to a servant," admonished her mother.

Puzzled, the child retreated to her small chair, looking to the elderly woman for comfort. A gnarled hand patted the child's fingers.

Joanna could feel her head spinning. The room seemed very warm after the cold outdoor air. How long since she'd been near a fire? She slipped her cloak from her shoulders, held it over her arm. She could see Mistress Gifford eying her saffron gown. Was her glance merely curious? Master Gifford too was regarding her closely.

"The first thing you must do, Margaret, is to get this girl some suitable clothing. She could be taken to court for wearing such lace." He flicked the cloak's gold trimming with his forefinger. "And her gown—of satin, no less, with a Flemish fall and virago sleeves! The fine would be vast. And you know well who'd be accountable for its payment."

His wife tapped her foot. "New clothes, even for a servant, cost money."

He shrugged his shoulders. "Better to pay the seamstress than the courts. This government is making me a pauper soon enough as it is, with its restrictions on the prices of iron. A man might prosper, would the lawmakers but leave him alone."

He looked out the window. Joanna followed his glance, caught a glimpse of the Scots grouped not far away.

"I must see to the placing of the new bondsmen," he said. "Had I had any inkling, when I accepted this post, that I'd have such trouble getting men to work here, I might have remained in England."

Joanna put her hand on the doorjamb for support. She could feel herself swaying.

"Margaret," said the white-haired dame, "why do you not take this young woman to the keeping room and give her something to eat? She must be tired after her journey."

Joanna threw her a grateful glance.

But Mistress Gifford spun resentfully about. "I wish you would remember, Mother, that this is my house and I am the one to make decisions."

Joanna could see the older woman flinch. Was there no end to the enmity in this household?

Despite her avowed independence, Mistress Gifford led Joanna across the hallway and through the doorway opposite, into the keeping room. Here were even more warmth and light, flowing from a huge hearth that took up half the center wall. Bunches of pennyroyal, catnip, and mullein hung from the ceiling. A dresser boasting rows of pewter plates stood against the wall. A table in the center of the room held wooden bowls and trenchers. In one corner, between a chest and cupboard, stood a low bed.

At the room's farther end, a stout woman rose slowly from her knees. Joanna could almost hear her joints creaking. One hand held a wet cloth, which she dropped into a wooden bucket at her feet.

"Have a care where you step," she cautioned sharply. "The floor is fresh scrubbed." Her tone held no hint of respect. Joanna waited for a word of reprimand from Mistress Gifford. But none was forthcoming.

"This is your new helper, Huldah," she said simply, then asked, "What is your name, girl?"

Still half giddy, Joanna told her. She longed to sit down till the dizziness passed, but it would be disrespectful for a servant to sit in the mistress's presence. If only Huldah would not stare at her so with her beady black eyes. A body would think she'd never seen a stranger before.

"Helper—faugh!" Huldah put both hands on her hips and made a grimace. "When will ye get me a decent wench? First a blackamoor that sickens and dies at the earliest frost, and now this fancy miss. Next thing 'twill be a Nipmuck squaw."

"Give her something to eat," said Mistress Gifford, ignoring Huldah's insolence, "and show her where she's to sleep, whilst I see to proper garb for her." She sailed from the room, her head high.

Joanna sank down on a stool in the corner of the room. How long before she became accustomed to the warmth of a house? And to the antagonism that crackled in the air here?

In a few moments Huldah thumped a wooden trencher onto the table, its contents steaming. Beside it she placed an iron spoon.

"Don't take it into your head that I'm going to wait on you all the time like this," she said.

Joanna picked up the spoon and dipped it into the stew. There was meat in it, there were onions, turnips, and dried beans. So tasty a dish she'd not eaten in months. After the *Unity's* cold salt beef and biscuits, the hot food tasted wondrously good. She had scarcely finished eating when the mistress returned with a bundle of clothing over her arm. She gave the garments to Joanna.

"These should fit you well enough," she said. "Goody Turner had them on hand and was glad to get rid of them. The bondmaid they were intended for died a fortnight ago."

"Died!" Huldah snorted. "Was killed, you mean."

"Killed?" asked Joanna.

Mistress Gifford nodded matter-of-factly. "A pack of wolves caught her at nightfall. She should have known better than to go any distance from the village."

Joanna shuddered. Not two weeks ago a girl had been killed by wild beasts, and now people could speak of it calmly. What manner of country was this New England?

She wished Huldah would show her to her room. What she wanted now was to be away from these strange voices and prying eyes, to be quiet and alone, and to have time to sort out her thoughts.

There came a scratching on the door. Wolves?

"That Ruff is more trouble than a child," grumbled Huldah. She lifted the latch and a Shetland sheep dog shot into the room, all black save for tan markings on his face and a white ruff around his neck. He approached Joanna on stiff legs, sniffing her suspiciously.

How good to see a dog again! Slowly she extended a hand, let the dog nose it. His tail began to wag, and he looked up at her happily, one black ear drooping, the other cocked rakishly. She longed to fall on her knees and bury her face in his fur. Instead she contented herself with rubbing his head behind the ears.

Mistress Gifford was speaking again. "Huldah," she said, "show Joanna where to find the washtub, and give her some water from the kettles. She'll not be fit for service here till she's rid of the shipboard stench. See to it that she bathes all over."

Huldah gave an audible snort, muttering, "A bath in the wintertime!"

Joanna could feel her face flushing with more than the heat of the fire. The worst of it was, Mistress Gifford was right. Who wouldn't stink—there was no other word for it —after six weeks in a smelly cabin, wearing the same garments day after day, nursing an ill man? And with no soap, and no water but what she'd drawn up over the side of the ship?

She rolled the wooden tub from the shed adjoining the kitchen and set it in a corner at one end of the hearth. She found the soap, brown and strong-smelling, in a barrel. Water she drew from the well, bucket by bucket, and poured it into the tub, warming it with the contents of the kettles. When all was ready, she pulled the high-backed settle across the corner and undressed in the space behind it.

When she had scrubbed herself until her skin smarted from the caustic soap, she wrapped herself in a towel and washed her hair. That was the best of all, to feel the salt stickiness dissolving, to rub her scalp until it tingled. A bucket of warm water she had set to one side served to rinse her hair. She could hear the wet strands squeak between her fingers. Vigorously she rubbed her head with a dry towel, then put on the new clothes Mistress Gifford had brought.

The coarse linen shift went on first. It was rough but would have to do. Then came a chemise of the same linen, a skirt of brown wool, and a bodice to match fastened down the front with black laces. Coarse green knit hose and rough shoes of calfskin covered her feet. She'd try to forget that her apparel had been fashioned for another, now dead and gone.

Standing in front of the fire, she dried her hair. How wonderful it was to be clean once more! She could even smile at Huldah.

But Huldah did not return the smile. She pointed wordlessly at the tub and buckets. Joanna emptied them outside and returned them to their places, while fatigue washed over her in great waves. She could hardly keep her eyes open; her hands and feet felt heavy. As from a great distance she heard Huldah say, "I doubt I'll get any work out of you tonight. I'll serve the supper by myself, and you can make up for it tomorrow. Your bed's in the garret. You can find it yourself."

In a daze Joanna stumbled up the stairs, carrying her satin gown and cloak over her arm, a Betty lamp in her hand. On the second-floor landing she unlatched the door to the garret and climbed the steep steps. Holding the lamp high, she found the bed—more nearly a cot, so low and narrow it was. Once, she would have deemed the straw mattress and coarse blankets far from acceptable. Tonight she thought she had never seen a more welcome sight. She hung her gown over a bench and slipped out of her clothing and into a tow night rail that had been in the bundle. The fur-lined cloak she spread over the blankets for added warmth, and gratefully crawled beneath the covers.

The glow from the smelting furnace showed crimson at the windows, casting weird shadows on the rafters overhead. The roar of the vast stack sounded eerie and mysterious. But she had time neither to think nor to be afraid. Almost at once she sank into a deep, dreamless sleep.

5

The Bondmaid's Day

While it was still dark, Joanna was roused by the sound of a horn. For a moment she thought she was back in England, the horn signaling the arrival of a stagecoach. Then the drawn-out notes receded, and she drifted back into slumber. The next thing she knew, a strong hand was shaking her. She opened her eyes to Huldah's scowl.

"Up, girl! The mistress brooks no slugabeds! Did you not hear the watch?"

Still half asleep, Joanna could only repeat stupidly, "The watch?" Brr, it was cold. She pulled the covers around her shoulders.

"All of half an hour ago he came past, a-blowing of his horn. 'Tis the signal for all to be up and stirring. If there's no light in the house when he comes back along the road, he'll report us."

Joanna could hardly believe her ears. "You mean all the Hammersmith folk must rise before daylight?"

Huldah nodded shortly. "And every house must be dark by nine of an evening, else the watch'll report 'em. Come along, now."

Dressing was a simple matter and a hurried one in the cold garret. Though coarse, the brown wool garments were warm. What would she do with her hair? When she tried to part it with the silver-backed comb, each strand clung to her fingers as if it were alive. It would never stay up with the few pins she had. Best plait it. If only she had a mirror and could see to do it neatly. Perhaps the glass in the casement would serve.

The view from the window was so engrossing she stared for long minutes, regardless of the biting cold. On the hillside below, workmen hurried toward the sheds of the Iron Works. At the crest of the hill smoke and sparks rose in a fiery cloud from the mouth of the great furnace. Men bearing baskets heaped with a black substance, and others trundling barrows laden with heavy chunks of material, advanced to a platform encircling the chimney and threw their burdens into its gaping maw. In the dim gray light, they might have been primitive worshipers making sacrifices to a god of fire.

Either the light was too dim or the glass not right; she couldn't see how she looked. No matter. She felt neat, at least. She tied her apron tightly about her waist and hurried down the stairs. She must hurry, or Huldah would be crosser than ever. Perhaps if she did her best to be cheerful and willing and helpful, Huldah might not be quite so unpleasant. She'd try.

When she entered the keeping room, Ruff greeted her with a wag of his tail, one ear cocked engagingly. Huldah was sweeping the hearth with a birch broom.

"Come in and bestir yourself, Miss Peacock," she said, without looking up. "There's a deal of work to be done."

Miss Peacock! Joanna could feel her fine resolutions exploding. Who could be friendly with such a bristling creature? Of course it was to be expected that Huldah would have heard how the Iron Master had greeted his new servant at the wharf. Perhaps if she spoke humbly . . .

"My name's Joanna," she said, trying to keep the resentment out of her voice. "I'd rather you called me that."

Huldah straightened and regarded her critically. "You've lost your peacock look," she admitted, "now that you're dressed more fitting. But you've still got your peacock air," she added critically. She swept the broom in a wide arc and ordered, "Now, my girl, do you make the corncake whilst I finish sweeping."

Corncake? Joanna didn't know what it was, let alone how to prepare it. "Perhaps you'd rather make the cake while I use the broom," she offered. "You know just how the master likes it."

"That's so," agreed Huldah.

Sweeping the shadowy corners of the room, Joanna watched the cook covertly. She took yellow meal from a wooden firkin, poured it in a bowl, mixed salt and milk with it, and a dollop of thick golden honey.

"A bit of sweetening makes it more tasty," she commented. From the hearth she took a round iron pan with four legs, greased it, and poured the yellow mixture in. On top she placed an iron cover with a wide cupped rim. After placing the pan over a bed of glowing coals, she heaped more coals on the cover.

"There," she said proudly. "I'll wager you've never seen a pan such as that."

"I have not," said Joanna honestly. If Huldah could guess how little she knew about pans of any sort!

"Most folk hereabout still bake their corncake on a stone or a shovel. But I dare say the Iron Master has better pots and pans than the governor himself. You'll see how fine that cooks—no ash, no cinders, just the good browned cake."

Joanna sniffed at the pots hungrily. There was porridge in one, thin gruel in another. Huldah was laying small smoked fish in a pan.

"Take care lest these burn," she cautioned, putting a fork in Joanna's hand.

Soon the fish were sizzling, sending up a tantalizing odor. "When do we eat our breakfast?" asked Joanna.

"After the master and mistress, of course. They'll be down soon. The corncake better be done in time. Mr. Gifford's not a patient man."

The Giffords came downstairs and sat at the table in the crimson-curtained great room. Even this early in the morning Mistress Gifford was imposing, every dark hair in place, her maroon dress showing not a wrinkle. Little Deborah sat quietly, her eyes bright with curiosity, but she spoke not a word. Joanna could feel those eyes upon her every time she entered the room. While Joanna served bowls of porridge, Huldah set the corncake before Mr. Gifford with a flourish. She had a right to be proud of it. The crust was golden brown. Joanna could feel her mouth watering.

Mr. Gifford took up a knife as if to cut the cake. His wife gave him a warning glance. He set the knife down, folded his hands, and intoned rapidly a brief blessing.

Though Joanna thought Mr. Gifford would eat corncake forever and there'd be none left, he finally finished, ending with a deep draft of cider. Then she could clear the table.

Back in the kitchen, Joanna took two pewter plates and set them on the table's scrubbed boards.

"And what fine folk be these for?" asked Huldah.

"For you and me. Are we not to have breakfast now?"

"Yes, but not off pewter. Wooden trenchers are good enough for us."

Joanna couldn't have relished the porridge more if she'd had a golden bowl to eat it from. The corncake was crisp on the outside, moist within, with a nutty flavor she found delicious. And the smoked fish had a salty tang that made her wish for more, but the pan was soon empty.

Only then did Joanna wonder about the other member of the family—the grandmother.

"Dame Forrest has her breakfast in bed, she's that lame," explained Huldah. "Her food is keeping hot in the covered plate on the hearth. She'll let us know when she wants it. Gives a rap on the floor with her cane."

Sure enough, a smart tap-tap soon sounded from the room above. Joanna carried the tray upstairs, knocked on the door of the south chamber, and entered. A large bed hung with green and violet curtains occupied the center of the room. Between two windows stood an intricately carved chest. At the other end of the room, pushed into a corner, was a spinning wheel, and beside it a towering loom, bright with the red and white threads of a half-woven piece of fabric.

A thin hand pushed back the bed hangings, and pale eyes looked out. Joanna bobbed in a half-curtsy and said,

"Good morrow, Dame Forrest." She couldn't help feeling, as she curtsied thus, taking care not to tip the tray, as if she were play-acting.

From the bed came a querulous voice. "Humph! There's nothing good about it. Another cold winter's day, and I shut in this house with naught to do nor friends to come calling. 'Twas an ill day when I left my brother's house in Devon." She paused a moment, then ordered, "Set the tray down, and help me up."

Joanna put her arms about the frail body. Heavens, the woman was little more than skin and bones. Gently she raised her, tucking a shawl around her shoulders and pillows at her back.

The fire was but a faint glow. She lifted a large log from a basket beside the hearth and laid it on the coals. A dry laugh came from the bed. "Put some kindling on first. It may burn then, especially if you give it a blow with the bellows."

Awkwardly Joanna did as she was bid. With some help from the bellows, the split pieces of wood burst into flame. Soon the fire was crackling and sending out heat into the chilly chamber.

"Have you ne'er mended a fire before?" asked Dame Forrest.

Joanna shook her head. "No," she admitted shamefacedly.

"Then you did not steal those clothes," crowed the dame triumphantly. "I told Margaret as much."

Joanna felt half sick from resentment. It was bad enough to be an orphan and penniless without being misjudged.

"Is there aught useful you know how to do?" inquired

the woman. "Can you spin or weave?" Her eyes went to the loom and wheel.

"No," said Joanna again, "though I can sew." No need to mention embroidery, or playing the harpsichord, or anything else impractical.

Dame Forrest had sunk back on her pillows, as if in disappointment. "I had hoped you could weave," she said. "In my day I had a certain skill, and I'd hoped to find someone to finish that coverlet on my loom. 'Tis for my granddaughter Deborah." She pushed the tray away. "You can take this now," she said in dismissal.

How she got through the rest of the day, Joanna never knew. Every minute she was kept busy. If it wasn't the mistress calling for fresh firewood, or Deborah requesting that she fasten the latchet on her shoe, it was Huldah telling her to chop onions for the stew. And not one thing could she seem to do right, not even so simple a thing as chopping onions.

She had taken the breadboard to cut them on, and was slicing them as neatly as she could, when Huldah snatched the board away, crying, "Not onions on this. They'll taint the bread." And she had handed her a smaller board, scarred and redolent of onion.

She'd come near to disaster in the making of bread too. Huldah had mixed and kneaded the brown mass and set it to rise on the settle in a wooden trough with a tight-fitting cover. After it had risen, she told Joanna to knead it again and form it into loaves.

Joanna plunged her hands into the spongy mass with confidence. But for some reason the dough that Huldah had handled with ease had turned into a sticky mess that clung to her fingers and palms with exasperating tenacity.

She struggled to no purpose until Huldah set a bowl of flour on the table beside her.

"Dip your hands in this," she suggested with more asperity than kindness.

From then on it had not been difficult, even pleasurable, to punch the dough, to press the heels of her hands against it, and to shape it into round loaves. At Huldah's bidding she set the loaves near the fire so that the warmth would aid their rising.

A few minutes later, noting that the flames were dying low, Joanna picked up a heavy log and started to put it on the fire. The wood slipped out of her grasp, fell among the glowing coals, and sent a shower of sparks and ashes flying high and wide. Sparks fell hissing into the bubbling kettle of stew. Bits of ash covered the half-risen loaves with black particles that clung to the dough. And cinders peppered a fowl roasting on a spit.

Huldah turned with an angry intake of breath. "You've ruined my good fire just as the coals were right for baking. Now we'll have to wait for the new log to burn down." She threw Joanna a baleful glance. "I hope you like cinders in your food. Nobody else does, and we'll hear about it."

In the afternoon a messenger from Salem came to the house with a document requiring the Iron Master's attention, and Joanna was sent to find him. In seconds she was out the door, blinking in the bright sunlight. How bracing the air was! And what a relief to be out of the house, if only for a few minutes. She looked toward the Iron Works. What a bustling, noisy place! Could she find the Iron Master amid the roaring confusion?

At the top of the hill, where men carried their burdens toward the huge chimney, she scanned the soot-streaked face of the man in charge. He looked up from the tally sheet in his hand.

"I'm looking for Mr. Gifford," she shouted above the chimney's roar.

"Try the casting shed." He pointed to broad stone steps set in the hillside. She ran down them, thankful to escape the acrid smoke. The steps led to the entrance of a tall wooden structure built about the chimney's base. When she first peered inside, her eyes still smarting, she could see only a gloomy cavern lit in one corner by a brilliant pool of fiery liquid. As her eyes adjusted, she made out a huge hearth. Where a fire would normally burn, a white-hot mass seethed and bubbled. Fiery drops fell into the glowing trough from the furnace above. Could this be molten iron in the making? To the right of the hearth a giant bellows heaved and wheezed. At the shed's open side a number of men were setting molds in sand.

"Have you seen Mr. Gifford?" she asked.

"He was here a while back. He might be at the forge."

She hurried on, past a gigantic water wheel, and stopped in the doorway of a large square building a few yards down the hillside. The noise was so deafening she had to put her hands over her ears. A gigantic hammer, its haft a tree trunk, rose and dropped with ear-splitting resonance. The iron head of the hammer, striking against a thick iron bar, produced the thundering racket. Swiftly she looked about at the leather-aproned, smoke-blackened men working red-hot lumps of iron at three open hearths. No one here even vaguely resembled the Iron Master.

Through the building she darted, ears tightly muffled, and came out on a bridge between two more water wheels. Beyond them was yet another building. She could see a man removing red-hot bars of iron from a furnace with heavy pincers and inserting the bars between two revolving iron rollers. Sparks flew from the hot metal. Just beyond she saw Mr. Gifford, his dark blue waistcoat and silver buttons incongruous in this setting.

Breathless, she gave him the message and watched him hurry toward the house. At a slower pace she followed, gazing about with eager eyes. What a strange, dirty, noisy place this was—and yet how fascinating.

Climbing the hill, she wondered what had become of the Scottish prisoners. In her hasty search through the Iron Works she'd been on the lookout for them as well as for Mr. Gifford, but had seen no sign of kilt or plaid. She'd have been glad to catch sight of one familiar face.

At the day's end, when the last plate had been set in the rack and the overnight log laid on the fire, Joanna sank down on a stool. She was weary to her very bones. For the life of her, she could not imagine how she could endure four years of days like this one. The work itself was exhausting. But the constant ordering about wore at her spirit even more.

By the light of a Betty lamp, Huldah was knitting, her thick fingers clumsily jabbing needles into wool. As she worked, her face wore its habitual frown. If good servants were as hard to come by as the Iron Master said, why did Huldah remain here in this unhappy household, cross and dissatisfied as she appeared? Was she, perhaps, indentured?

In a moment she had asked, "Are you a bond servant, Huldah?"

Huldah dropped her knitting in her lap. She raised her

small dark eyes, the dark brows forbidding. "That I am not, nor ever was," she retorted vehemently.

"Then why do you stay here?" The question was out almost before Joanna knew it.

Huldah gave her a look as if to say she'd better mind her own business. Then she said slowly, "Because this keeping room is mine, seems like."

Was that why Mistress Gifford kept to the rest of the house, hardly setting foot into this room?

"It's been home to me, you might say," Huldah went on, "since I came to these parts four years ago with Mr. Leader, him that was Iron Master afore Mr. Gifford. 'Twas for him this house was built, but it suited neither him nor his wife, so he built a grand mansion in Boston. He left me here to care for this house and to cook his meals when he came. Sometimes he'd stay for weeks at a time."

"Where is he now?" asked Joanna.

"Gone to a place up north, Berwick, 'tis called. He'd an idea for a sawmill with twenty saws all working at once. Think of it! A great one he was for new things, always drawing plans for machines, and keeping the men working till all hours. He was a hard man to work for, though."

"Was he cross?" She'd almost said "like Mr. Gifford."

"No, easygoing enough. But he would never get to his meals on time, always so wrapped up in his plans he'd forget to eat. Many's the night I've kept supper warming till it dried out like Indian meat."

"Why didn't you go to Berwick?" Surely a servant so trusted would be invited.

"I liked it here." Her eyes roved over the room, almost in contentment. She heaved herself to her feet. "The watch will soon be coming by. Best get to bed whilst you can have a light."

Joanna could hardly stand, she was so tired. Slowly she dragged herself upstairs. She was too fatigued even to think, though her mind was filled with questions about this new land. By the time the notes of the watchman's horn sounded outside, she was fast asleep and beyond hearing anything.

6

The Meetinghouse

"There, that should keep us from going hungry on the Sabbath." Huldah placed a roasted chicken on the table beside flaky meat pasties and a bowl of succotash.

"The Sabbath?" echoed Joanna. She'd lost all track of time in the few days she'd been at Hammersmith.

"Why else would I be doing this extra cooking, save for the Lord's Day?" inquired Huldah.

The Puritans must be very strict in their observance, thought Joanna. She'd heard they frowned on unnecessary labor on Sunday, but wasn't the preparing of food considered a necessity?

"Naught but cold meals tomorrow," said Huldah, as if in answer to her thought, a tinge of regret in her tone.

"At least you'll have a rest," offered Joanna, thinking gratefully that she would too.

Huldah said nothing. But the expression on her broad face cast doubt over Joanna's dream of a day of leisure.

The Sabbath began much as any other day, save that

breakfast, usually a hot, tasty meal, was cold and unpalatable. Then Joanna must take Dame Forrest's tray to her and help her into her clothes. The dame's fingers were so knotted she had difficulty with laces and buttons. When she was dressed, and a fresh cap on her head, she needed assistance descending the stairs. By the time she was settled in her chair by the fire, with Ruff lying on the floor beside her, the Giffords and Huldah were donning their warm cloaks. Joanna hurried to fetch hers, an old russet one of Mistress Gifford's with the trim removed. Though of wool, it was not nearly so warm as her own, she realized regretfully once she stepped outside into the winter air.

All up and down the street Hammersmith folk were leaving their homes or were already on the way to meeting. Families walked in sober groups, fathers and mothers in the lead, children and servants straggling behind.

So it was with the Giffords. The master and mistress walked ahead. Behind them trudged Deborah, her short legs pumping. Then came Huldah and beside her Joanna, carrying Mistress Gifford's footstove, a square iron receptacle that held hot coals from the fire. Though it was an awkward burden, needing to be held out from her cloak lest it scorch the cloth, she was glad for the warmth it gave out.

The meetinghouse little resembled the churches Joanna had known in England. A square frame building, it had small windows set high in the walls. Within, it was dull and cheerless, with rows of wooden benches on a rough plank floor. And it was cold, with the penetrating chill of a building never heated. No wonder the mistress wanted a footstove. Joanna would have liked one for herself.

From the narrow bench on which she and Huldah sat

near the back, Joanna could see Mistress Gifford, majestic in her high-crowned hat, in the front row. As the wife of the Iron Master, she had one of the choice places. On either side of her were ranged the wives of leading men, clad in gleaming silks and satins. One had a cloak of scarlet, another had one of brilliant blue. Here, as in England, their wealth and rank were reflected in their costumes despite laws restricting the richness of dress.

The men in the front benches were garbed in equal elegance. In the rows between were ranged farmers and merchants, in more sober clothing of good durable wool or kersey, as were their wives, sitting behind the ladies of importance. At the very back were the servants, Joanna among them, in rough practical garb.

Had the Scottish prisoners come to the meeting? At first glance, Joanna thought not, seeing no sign of tartan anywhere. The men on the last two benches across from her were clad alike in loose-fitting breeches of brown woolen cloth, with leather doublets topping rough wool shirts. Their hair was cut short, and their faces were clean-shaven. Then a head turned her way, with dark hair crisp and shining, the eyes searching. It was Ross McCrae, oddly unfamiliar. She could see his face lighten for an instant as his eyes met hers.

The benches were nearly all filled when a woman entered, paused a moment inside the door, then walked with unhurried grace to a place directly in front of the pulpit.

" 'Tis the minister's wife, Mistress Whiting," whispered Huldah.

The garnet of Mistress Whiting's cloak heightened the bright color in her cheeks. The beaver fur of her hood and muff was only a shade lighter than the smooth waves of her hair. Her eyes sparkled with warmth and intelligence, and her lips were parted in a smile that seemed to embrace the entire congregation. Behind her in single file came three girls.

Joanna recognized them instantly. Ever since the day she arrived, she had been wondering about the Indian girl, hoping she might see her again. She watched as the trio made their way down the aisle behind the minister's wife, the copper-skinned girl walking between the two sisters.

Soon the minister appeared and mounted the pulpit. Of a slender build, he had fine, even features, soft gray hair falling just below his ears, and a narrow beard trimmed to a point. On his head was a black cap; white linen bands topped his flowing black cassock.

He had cleared his throat, as if about to speak, when the door opened and a strange figure entered. The minister waited. A tall middle-aged Indian strode down the aisle, his feet noiseless in leather moccasins, his limbs encased in deerskin leggings. Upon his head was a high beaver hat, about his shoulders a red blanket edged with shells, thrown back to display a lace-trimmed coat of canary yellow. He made his way to a bench near the front, gestured to the occupants to move over, and sat down. He then looked toward the minister with an expectant glance.

Who was this savage so bizarrely clad? He must be a person of importance. But who? Might there be some connection between him and the Indian girl? Joanna stole a glance in her direction but could see only the back of her crimson cloak and hood.

The service began with a long prayer. Then came a Psalm. After that came the sermon. For all that Mr.

Whiting had not a robust appearance, he had tremendous stamina when it came to preaching. The sermon went on and on.

In front of her, Joanna could see heads nodding, but not for long. A short spindly man stalked up and down the aisles, carrying a long pole. On one end was a foxtail, on the other a wooden knob. Now and again the man would swish the fur against the cheek of a sleeper. The head would jerk, and the spine straighten.

Joanna grew stiff and cold. She tried to shift her position on the narrow hard bench, but Huldah threw her a forbidding frown. Her feet grew icy. She drew the russet cloak about her, but its folds gave little comfort.

At last the sermon came to an end. There was another Psalm; then Joanna could thankfully follow Huldah outside. Once there, she almost fled back into the meetinghouse, terrified, for gathered on the opposite side of the road was a score or more of Indians.

Furs of wild animals were thrown over their deerskin garments; their right arms were encased in pelts of fox or lynx. Some wore feathers in their hair; others had bits of shining metal hung about their necks. Though Joanna watched them with trepidation, no other member of the congregation seemed alarmed. Apparently they were accustomed to this group of savages stolidly regarding them as they left the meetinghouse.

One Indian youth stood apart from the others. He held his head proudly, an eagle feather twisted in his long black hair, and appeared to be searching the crowd for someone in particular. As the Whiting family came out of the meetinghouse, the Indian maiden with them, he stepped forward eagerly.

At a word from Mistress Whiting, the copper-cheeked girl went to meet him. For a few minutes they spoke earnestly. When she returned to the minister's family, her face was calm, betraying no expression. Yet one hand went up to her eye, as if swiftly brushing away a tear.

To Joanna's disappointment, there was no opportunity for her to say even a word to the Scots. She noticed that they set off almost immediately after the service in a different direction from the village, taking a cart track through the woods.

Last of the congregation to emerge was the bizarrely clad Indian. He hesitated in the doorway, regarding the assembled braves suspiciously. Then, gathering his blanket about him, he strode forward between the knots of chatting people.

A stern-visaged man standing nearby said loudly, "If that stinking Wapaket sits near me again, I shall complain to Mr. Whiting. I helped build this meetinghouse, and I pay my share of the minister's salary. I've got my place assigned to me, and I'll have no savage thinking he's as good as Obadiah Talbot. Why don't he sit in back with the servants? Or stay outside like the other redskins?"

There was a murmur of approval from those about him.

Huldah raised her voice. "I don't see what call the Indian girl has to sit up front with Mistress Whiting. When us decent white women with spirit enough to work for a living have to sit in back! What say you, Goody Talbot? Like you to see a heathen take a place meant for wives of freemen and important folk?"

Goody Talbot pursed her thin lips, saying, "I never did hold with the minister taking that girl in." She had a shallow forehead and dark brows that grew together in the middle, as if in a perpetual frown.

"And I don't want any part of my money going to feed an Indian," her husband said.

The Giffords appeared and gestured to Huldah and Joanna. Soon they were walking briskly along the road. Obviously upset, Mr. Gifford was talking loudly, his voice clearly audible.

"Of all the ridiculous things, a praying Indian is the worst! It may make a fine godly sentiment for men safely in England to say that the converting of the heathen shall be one of the colony's purposes. 'Tis another thing to live here with the savages at one's elbow, never knowing when they may erupt in violence. This morning's scene was disgusting. I can still smell that rancid bear's grease on Wapaket! Faugh!"

Joanna slowed her pace until she and Huldah had dropped several paces behind the Giffords. Then she asked Huldah, "Why are people so set against the Indians?"

Huldah replied sourly, "Mr. Whiting has a fool idea that he can make the Indians into honest, God-fearing people. Everyone knows they'd as soon steal as eat. They're just naturally lazy and dirty and no-account. And ignorant. But the minister spent a lot of time teaching Wapaket until he said he believed in Jesus. Now Wapaket goes around telling white men that the Bible says this and the Bible says that. He even told Obadiah Talbot he shouldn't chop wood on Sunday."

"Is it lawful?" asked Joanna. Certainly chopping wood was work, and all work was forbidden on the Sabbath.

"Well, a man couldn't let his family go cold for want of

wood," protested Huldah. "And that isn't all. Wapaket brought his daughter Yaweta to Mr. Whiting and gave her to him so she could learn to be a Christian. Of all the nonsense! Poor Mistress Whiting had to take that savage into her home, with her innocent little girls. But she's a saint, Mistress Whiting is. She never lets on how frightened she is of Yaweta, or disgusted with her wild ways. You saw how she's dressed, better than some white girls. And she has a seat in the foremost pew, as if she *was* somebody."

Yaweta. The musical name kept singing itself over and over in Joanna's mind. The girl seemed quiet and docile. Was she really as savage as Huldah had intimated?

After the brisk walk back from the meetinghouse, even the cold meal was welcome at noon. So was the fire, freshened with sticks of kindling. Too soon it was time for the afternoon service. The footstove seemed heavier now. Deborah lagged behind her parents and tugged at Joanna's free hand.

The afternoon service was as long as the morning's. For his text the minister chose Matthew 25:35. "For I was an hungered, and ye gave me meat: I was thirsty, and ye gave me drink: I was a stranger, and ye took me in."

These words from the Bible were some the people of Hammersmith would do well to follow, said Mr. Whiting. Joanna sat up, filled with new interest. She was a stranger; she knew what it was to be hungry. When the minister adjured his congregation to open their homes and hearts to the strangers within their gates, she was sure he was referring to the Scots and to herself. Then he began to speak of those who were hungering for the word of Christ, how they should be welcomed into the Church, and she thought he must mean the Indians. She never was quite sure which he meant, but she followed every word thankfully.

In the middle of the sermon, loud snores resounded through the building. The tithing man circled about until he located the sleeper, a stout man at the end of a bench, leaning against the wall. The foxtail flourished; the sleeper merely stirred. The tithing man reversed the pole and hit the sleeper's head a sharp blow. Instantly the man jumped up with a loud curse. For a moment he stood in confusion, his face brick-red, then sank down on the bench.

"His fine will doubtless be doubled for cursing in meeting," said Huldah in Joanna's ear with malicious pleasure.

For the remainder of the service there was no more nodding.

Again the Indian maiden sat with the Whitings. Joanna felt her eyes drawn to her again and again. Was Yaweta happy as a member of the minister's family? Had she had any voice in the decision, or had she been handed over like a chattel, a bondmaid? Joanna studied the proud set of the dark head. How she would like to know the thoughts within it!

7

The River

"I'm going to Goodwife Thaxter's this afternoon," announced Mistress Gifford to her mother as Joanna cleared the table after the noonday meal a few days later. "If she can let out this violet kersey satisfactorily, I'll have her make up my new green lustring. I've heard she has some skill with the needle and pray it may be true. My wardrobe is in a sorry state."

"The whole family's as well," added Dame Forrest, dourly regarding the torn banding on her sleeve. "Could you but ply a needle—"

"Oh, Mother, you know I've no skill with my fingers." Mistress Gifford's tone was cross.

Debby jumped up from her stool. "May I go with you, Mamma? May I?" Her hazel eyes were round and pleading, her soft curls bobbing on her shoulders.

"No, Deborah, you will remain at home. Joanna will look after you."

"Please, Mamma."

"No coaxing, Deborah." Her tone was adamant. She looked toward Joanna, whose hands were laden with plates. "Do what Dame Forrest bids you, and help Huldah with the evening meal," she ordered.

Joanna left the room, fuming. Why did Mistress Gifford have to give one order after another, and more often than not unnecessarily? Of course she'd do what Dame Forrest bade her. Of course she'd help Huldah prepare the supper. Did the mistress think she would sit in a corner with Debby and play with her poppet all afternoon?

No sooner had Mistress Gifford departed by the front door than Huldah went out the back. Her shoulder was bothering her something terrible; she needed some ointment for it. Goody Jenks had something that did wonders. She'd got it from an Indian medicine man, and it was worth the wool tippet she'd given him, though she did think it funny every time she saw him wearing it over his deerskin.

Dame Forrest decided that today was a good time to turn out the oaken chest in her chamber. Joanna helped her make her painful way up the stairs, with Debby crowding close and nearly causing them all to fall. Joanna built up the fire, for the room was chill. Then she pulled the wing chair close to the chest and helped the elderly woman into it.

The cover of the chest was heavy and would not stay open of itself. She propped it up with a stick. The fragrance of lavender rose in a wave, filling the room. Inside the chest were coverlets the dame had woven herself. There were sheets and bolster slips of her own weaving as well. Underneath were petticoats, stiff and quilted. There were gowns, ruffed and stomachered brocades of the reign of Queen Bess. Over each one the dame sighed and reminisced in her dry, thin voice. As Joanna stooped to pick up a set of bed hangings, stiff with embroidery, from the bottom of the chest, she saw Debby grasp the prop stick, asking, "What might this be for?"

Quick as a flash, before she could dislodge the stick, Joanna hit the small hand a smart blow.

"Don't touch that," she said sharply. "The lid might fall down." She was lucky the cover hadn't fallen and broken her neck.

Debby began to sob, nursing her hand. "You slapped me," she cried. "You're bad." She ran from the room, tears running down her cheeks.

Joanna stood irresolute. The poor child had only wanted some attention. She was about to follow her and comfort her when Dame Forrest said impatiently, "You can put these back now. I'm tired and wish to rest."

She was not too tired, however, to direct in minute detail the return of her treasures to the chest. Then there was the task of getting her downstairs again. Debby was not in the great room. Probably she was in the keeping room, playing with Ruff.

Neither girl nor dog was in the keeping room. There was no sound save the purr of the low fire and the distant rumble and clang of the Iron Works, so much a part of life here Joanna was scarcely conscious of it now.

Had Debby gone to her parents' bedchamber? Joanna flew up the stairs, her anxiety quickening. No, she was not there, or in the porch chamber, or even in the garret.

In the entry, Joanna saw that the child's scarlet cloak was gone. Snatching up her own, she flung a quick word of explanation to Dame Forrest and ran out the door.

Outside she paused uncertainly. On her left lay the Iron Works, teeming with activity, noisy with the strike of iron upon iron. Somewhere in that smoky racket was Mr. Gifford. Would Debby go to him? Probably not.

In the other direction was the village, its road following the curve of the river. Among the houses was Goody Thaxter's. Debby would be more likely to seek out her mother to complain of her ill usage. If Joanna hurried, she might find her before she reached the Thaxter house.

She passed a row of small, steep-pitched houses occupied by ironworkers and their families. Beyond lay larger, more scattered dwellings belonging to other residents, farmers for the most part. From each stout chimney, smoke spiraled upward, but there was no other sign of life. Small wonder no one was abroad. The sky was gray and threatening, the air filled with a damp chill that pierced to the bone. Ahead stretched the empty road. There was no sign of Deborah or of any other living creature.

Soon she came to a fork in the road. Nailed to a tree was a board with the word *Boston* painted on it, and an arrow pointing to the right. An idea came to her mind with dazzling clarity. Her heart leaped with excitement. She would run away!

No one would miss her for an hour or more, and by then she would be well away from Hammersmith—away from the keeping room with its never-ending tasks, away from crochety Huldah, from haughty Mistress Gifford and demanding Dame Forrest. Even away from Debby.

At that instant she heard the bark of a dog. Below on the river bank was a flash of scarlet—Debby's cloak. The child had a long stick in her hand and was poking at the ice that edged the water. Could Debby have seen her?

Joanna was sure not. And Ruff? For one agonizing moment he cocked his head in her direction, then took Debby's stick in his jaws and tugged at it.

Through the leafless trees Joanna could dimly see a large frame house, but there was no sign of any inhabitant. Picking up her long skirts, she broke into a run, her feet skimming over the frozen ground, her heart beating with excitement. Every minute counted. She must make the most of the time.

She had gone perhaps half a mile when the thought struck her. In her mind's eye she could see the dog tugging at the stick. Was he trying to draw Debby away from the river? The banks were steep, she remembered. Covered with ice, they'd be treacherous. What if the child should slip and fall in?

Joanna slowed her steps. Should she give up this chance to find freedom? A wetting would do Debby no harm. It would teach her a lesson to stay away from the river. But the water was deep and the current strong. Could Debby get out by herself? Oh, why had Joanna been cursed with an imagination and a conscience? She would never have a peaceful moment if she kept on now, not knowing what might befall Debby. If the child should come to harm, she'd never forgive herself.

She turned about and began to retrace her steps. This time fear spurred her on. She was tired, and her breath came in gasps, but she must hurry. What if the child should drown?

At the fork of the road she slowed her steps, sighing with relief. Debby was in almost the same spot, still poking at the ice. Why had Joanna been such a fool as to come back? Furious at herself, she picked her way down the hillside to the river. So long as she had given up the chance to get away, she might as well take Debby home.

At her approach, Ruff bounded to meet her, barking sharply. Debby turned and in one swift movement slipped, fell, and slid down the bank into the river.

At once Joanna was racing down the hill. Bushes caught at her skirt; brambles tore at her cloak. She ran on, her heart pounding, her eyes on the small red figure struggling in the water. At the riverbank she picked up the stick and held it toward the child.

"Catch hold, Debby," she cried, thrusting it out as far as she could.

Debby grasped the branch, her face twisted with fear. Her wet fingers slipped, and she tumbled over backward, her head sinking beneath the water.

In a moment Joanna had slid down the bank and into the water. It was no more than waist-high, but so icy that the shock nearly stunned her. She caught hold of Debby, pulled her to her feet, and shoved her toward the bank. Her one thought was to get out of the water. Her feet and legs were already numb with the cold. She tried to push Deborah up the bank, but the child could only claw futilely at the icy slope.

"Take hold of the reeds," ordered Joanna. The water was dragging at her skirts, pulling her out into the stream. And Deborah was heavy, her soaked garments adding to her weight.

"I can't get up," sobbed Debby as the rushes broke in her hands.

"Let me try, then. Hold on to me and don't let go."

Joanna let Debby slide down beside her, waited till she could feel the child's arms firmly about her waist. Then she attempted to climb out. She could almost get a footing. But each time she tried to heave herself out of the water the weight of the child held her back. Alone, she might get out and run for help. But if she left Debby for an instant the small girl might be swept away.

The water was rising with the incoming tide. She couldn't keep her footing much longer. Already she was so numb she could scarcely move. How ridiculous to perish within an arm's reach of safety! She had nearly given up hope when a figure appeared on the bank above. A stout sapling came within her grasp.

There was not a minute to waste. Taking a firm hold on the wood, Joanna gave a spring of desperation. She was out of the water. She was on her knees, part way up the bank, Debby clinging like a limpet to her back. She started to slip. Then her toe found a crack in the ice, enough to check her slide. She kept fast hold on the sapling and gave a tremendous push with the foot in the crack. Then hands caught at her shoulders, pulling her upward. Clawing at the frozen earth, she scrabbled onto level ground and lay there, gasping, Debby still plastered to her back.

They had been there no more than a minute when Debby was pulled up and Joanna helped to her feet. Only then did Joanna look at her rescuer. It was Yaweta.

A sob burst from Joanna. "How can I ever thank you?" she asked, clinging to the Indian girl's hands.

Debby began to cry. Yaweta said, "There is no need to thank me, but you must come to the house before you freeze."

Together Joanna and Yaweta half dragged, half lifted

Debby up the hillside. Ruff bounded beside them, barking lustily. In a few minutes they reached the road and the frame house Joanna had seen earlier. The Indian girl hurried them to the door, opened it, and pushed them inside. Instantly they were in a world of warmth and firelight.

Hours later Joanna awoke from a deep sleep. Beside her she could feel Debby's warm little body, hear her soft, regular breathing. Mistress Whiting had insisted on putting them into the best bed in the great room, where a brisk fire burned. She had given them night rails, smooth and scented with rose petals. She had made them each drink a hot potion, sweet yet tangy, that held drowsiness in every drop. And she had sent a message to the Giffords that they were safe and would spend the night at her home.

Beside the bed Ruff stirred. Joanna reached down to pat his head. He rose, licked her hand, then stretched out again. If Ruff had not run barking to the Whitings' house . . . if Yaweta, drawing water from the well, had not run with him to the river. . . . Despite the warmth of the bed, Joanna shuddered at what might have happened.

In the firelight she could see the door to the hallway crack open. Mistress Whiting, a candle in her hand, peered in.

"Ah, you're awake. And hungry too, no doubt." Her voice was low and soft. She went to a chest in a corner, pulled from it a fleecy garment, and held it to the fire a few minutes, then came to the bedside. "Here. Put this on and come with me."

Joanna slid from the bed, careful not to waken Debby. Ruff opened one eye and watched her as she left.

Before the keeping-room fire Mistress Whiting had drawn two stools, a low table between them. Over a bed of coals she warmed a pipkin of milk and toasted slices of bread. These she set before Joanna with cheese and cherry jam. The rest of the family had been abed an hour or more, she said—Yaweta too.

Taking a cup of hot milk for herself, she sipped slowly as Joanna ate. The food was delicious, but Joanna hardly tasted it, so overwhelmed was she by Mistress Whiting's tender ministration. Was this a dream from which she would soon awaken and find herself in her garret cot?

She had scarcely finished eating when Mistress Whiting fixed a sorrowful gaze upon her and said, "Joanna, what must you be thinking of me? I am filled with contrition for my neglect."

"Neglect?" She'd given Joanna more kindly attention than she'd had in months.

Mistress Whiting nodded. "On the Sabbath—and after my husband's sermon, too. I should have welcomed you then, spoken some word of friendship."

Surely this was a dream. No one in the Gifford household had spoken to her with such friendliness. But the warm voice continued. "I recall so well my own first Sabbath in this country. 'Twas a winter's day, and I thought I had never seen so bleak and desolate a spot. I felt I could not bear to remain. All I could think of was escape."

Joanna listened wordlessly.

"I even started off one time," Mistress Whiting went on.

"'Twas a cheerless day, with no other soul abroad. I shall never forget it."

"But you came back," said Joanna.

"Yes, I suddenly realized that I wasn't running *to* another place, but *away from* this one. I'd no plan, no purpose, save leaving behind my duties. So I came back. Those two miles were the longest and hardest I'd ever journeyed. I fought myself every step of the way."

"How well I know," breathed Joanna. In a moment she was telling of her own struggle that afternoon, pouring out her stored-up sorrow, bitterness, and resentment.

Mistress Whiting listened, her eyes dark pools of sympathy. Joanna told her everything—her mother's illness and death, the attack by Cromwell's men, her father's burial at sea, and her indenture. When she had finished, the tears were streaming down her cheeks and she was sobbing in Mistress Whiting's arms.

When finally she had wiped her eyes, she heard Mistress Whiting say, her voice uneven with emotion, "Joanna Sprague, I am vastly proud of you. How magnificently you have faced up to problems that would have felled a lesser woman."

Could she believe her ears? After her tears had proved how weak she truly was?

"You have shown true courage, nursing your father on that long voyage, and binding yourself to pay his debt— and today most of all."

"I really didn't stop to think. *Anyone* would have jumped in after Debby."

"Of course that took courage," said Mistress Whiting. "But 'twas your decision to turn back that took the most strength. And was your salvation, too."

"My salvation?"

The minister's wife nodded. "Last winter a woman was frozen to death on the road from Lynn to Boston. Her body was found in the spring where she'd sat down to rest in the shelter of a rock. A few weeks ago a young bond-maid was torn to pieces by wolves. Indians sometimes attack wayfarers. And there are those who turn runaway servants over to the authorities. You know what happens to those who are caught, do you not?"

"Are they reprimanded?" She could imagine the scolding Mistress Gifford would give her.

"They're set in the stocks and publicly whipped."

"Not women, surely!"

"Yes, girls and women, as well as men. Thirty-nine lashes is the usual number. Then a year is added to the culprit's term of service."

Joanna winced, and Mistress Whiting continued thoughtfully, "I'm sure you realized too, when you turned back, that, no matter how pleasant a situation you might find, you'd always be in fear of being found out."

It was true. Now that she could think clearly, she knew that running away was not the answer. She would have to remain at Hammersmith, where her duty lay. She would have to work out her debt. Then and there she abandoned all thought of flight.

Mistress Whiting was speaking again, her eyes still thoughtful. "Truly the Lord sent you to the Giffords."

The Lord? It seemed more as if the devil had pushed her into that situation. And the Giffords had certainly not regarded her as heaven-sent.

"Yes, they have need of someone like you. Have you

ever seen a home where love is more lacking? Poor little Debby is starved for it, and Dame Forrest is shriveling away for want of it. From what you have said, I know your family life was rich in happiness. Some day you will marry and make a home of your own, where your strength and devotion will give heart to others. In the meantime, you have the Giffords."

Joanna sighed. Yes, she had the Giffords. It was all right for Mistress Whiting, safe and assured by her own fireside, to regard them with tolerance and charity. She might think differently if she were to live one day in the Iron Master's house.

Mistress Whiting was continuing. "There's another who has need of someone like you."

Joanna gave her a questioning glance.

"Yaweta." Mistress Whiting's expression was pensive. "It is hard for her to live here with us. Everything is new and different for her—this house, her clothes, our food, and our prayers. We try to bring her into our family circle, to treat her as our own daughter. But she is lonely."

"I cannot fathom how anyone could be lonely here," said Joanna. She felt almost jealous of Yaweta because she lived under the Whitings' roof. "Besides, I do not know how I could help Yaweta." Had Mistress Whiting forgotten that she was a bond servant, kept to her tasks every hour of the day?

The minister's wife was smiling. "You'll find a way. I've great faith in you, Joanna." She rose, her eyes bright in the firelight. "Now we'd best be getting to bed. Let me light you the way."

In the snug four-poster bed, Joanna could see again in

her mind's eye the gracious figure preceding her, candle held high.

Had Mistress Whiting an inkling of how much more she was lighting for her than the way into a dark room?

8

The Scorched Cuff

Had Joanna expected any word of thanks from the Giffords for her part in rescuing Debby from the river, she would have been sorely disappointed. Though Mistress Gifford snatched Debby to her in an unwonted show of affection, she could only scold her bond servant. Why had she allowed Debby to leave the house? After Joanna had been so clumsy as to fall into the water, why had she not come straight home instead of bothering the Whitings? It was bad enough that the minister himself had brought word of the accident. He had also reported that Yaweta was the one who had pulled the girls out. Now he would expect the Giffords to express some gratitude to the young squaw. As if that were likely!

Joanna could overlook a lack of appreciation for herself, but not for the Indian girl. "We might both have perished, had it not been for Yaweta," she protested.

"Nonsense! You would have got out somehow." Mistress Gifford dismissed the matter.

Never had the Iron Master's house seemed more cheerless than it did now. Joanna's mind went back to breakfast at the Whitings' a short time ago, when the entire family had gathered about the big table. The minister's prayer had been far from perfunctory. He'd thanked the Lord for His mercy in sparing the lives of Joanna and Debby, and especially for His wisdom in sending Yaweta to their aid.

Her heart nearly bursting with gratitude, Joanna had lifted her head and looked straight into Yaweta's dark eyes. For a moment their glances locked. Surely she had not imagined the promise of friendship in that gaze. She could still see the soft curve of Yaweta's tawny cheek, the beaded band encircling her head, and the crimson scarf that brightened her gown.

She was jerked back to the present by Mistress Gifford's sharp voice. "Don't stand there dawdling, Joanna. Help Debby off with her things, and then go into the keeping room. Huldah's in need of aid." She swept from the room and mounted the staircase.

Choking with resentment, Joanna began to unfasten Debby's cloak. If Mistress Whiting could be here and see how hopeless the situation was, she might be less confident of what changes Joanna could bring about. She had untied the knot of Debby's hood and was about to take it off when the little girl threw her arms tight about Joanna's neck and gave her a fervent kiss.

Joanna almost fell over backward in her surprise. Debby's face was lighted by a beatific smile. "I like you, Joanna," she said. "I care not that you are a bondmaid."

For one moment Joanna responded to the child's warmth. The next, stung to the quick, she pushed her away. "I wasn't born a bondmaid, you know," she said, and went to hang up the cloak. She'd hardly taken a step before she recalled Mistress Whiting's voice: Poor little Debby is starved for love. Perhaps she was not too late. She hurried back into the room and found Debby weeping over her doll wrapped in a grimy silk handkerchief.

Kneeling down, Joanna put a tentative arm about the child. "I like you too," she said, smiling into the woebegone face.

Debby brightened immediately. "My poppet wants to kiss you," she said, poking the doll against Joanna's cheek. "Now you kiss the poppet," she ordered, holding it up expectantly.

Joanna gave a dutiful peck to the wooden face. "Mercy me!" she exclaimed. "Your poppet must be cold. Has she no better clothes than this?"

Debby regarded the handkerchief sadly. "I have been trying to find a seamstress," she said in perfect imitation of her mother, "but 'tis difficult."

Into Joanna's mind flashed a picture of the small leather trunk filled with dolls' clothes she'd played with as a child.

"Some day," she promised, "when I can take time, I'll make your poppet a gown."

"A real one, with sleeves and buttons?" Debby's eyes were like stars.

"A real one. And perhaps you can help make it." Hadn't she taken her first stitches on such garments? And how proud she had been of them!

In the middle of the night Joanna awoke to the roaring of wind and rattle of casements. Heavy gusts shook the rafters. For a moment she thought she was back on the *Unity*, its timbers creaking in a heavy sea. Then faint squares of dim light at the windows, and the dry homely fragrance of the house reassured her. She pulled her bed closer to the warmth of the chimney's great bulk, burrowed deep into the covers, and slept again.

Much later she woke with a guilty start. The light was stronger now. Had she slept through the notes of the watchman's rising horn? She tiptoed to the window, shivering as her bare feet struck the cold boards. Some snow had sifted in beneath the casement, and the small diamond-shaped panes were frosted. Breathing on the glass, she made a peephole and looked out. All she could see was swirling snow. Not even the watch would venture out in a storm like this.

In the keeping room Huldah had just risen from her bed in the corner. Ruff was stretching, his jaws wide in a yawn. Joanna put kindling and a fresh log on the fire, fanned the coals with a gentle puff from the bellows. Flames sprang up along the edges of the wood, crackling and sputtering as they licked at the sap. There was a satisfaction in building up a fire. It seemed to give off a better heat when she herself had worked on it.

Huldah groaned, tying a fresh apron over her dress. "A miserable kind of day, this," she complained. "Dark and dismal, and people tracking in the wet."

She'd hardly finished speaking when there was a stamping outside in the shed. The door opened to admit John Butt, the handy man, whitened with snow. In each hand he carried a bucket of milk, which he set down clumsily, slopping some on the table. He went out, leaving a pool of melted snow where he had stood. Huldah mopped at it fiercely. A minute later he was back again, his arms laden with wood, which he set down beside the hearth. A few trips more he made, then said, "That should do for today, but the woodpile's getting low."

All morning the blizzard continued, beating against the window panes, buffeting the house with strong gusts. While snow and wind raged without, other storms raged within.

Mistress Gifford had gone to bed the night before out of sorts, and this morning her temper was no better. Goodwife Thaxter's sewing had proved a disappointment. Now Mistress Gifford would have to begin hunting for another seamstress.

Dame Forrest was miserable because the storm made her rheumatism worse. No matter how close she sat to the fire, the drafts and dampness made her poor bones ache. Her knotted hands were clasped in her lap, her eyes fixed sadly on the flames. If only her fingers had not lost their suppleness she might be weaving or spinning instead of sitting idle.

The Iron Master, coming in from outside, shaking snow from his coat and stamping his boots, was furious that the storm had come. He had counted on a few weeks more for making iron. Why hadn't the cold weather held off, instead of freezing up the sluices and canals so no water could flow through them and keep the wheels in motion? People thought all an iron works needed was ore and flux and charcoal. But nothing could be accomplished without water to furnish power.

He disappeared into the office, returned a minute later, rubbing his hands. "I'll work in here today," he said. "It's so cold out there the ink won't run." He worked quietly for a few minutes, then looked up. "Is my dark blue coat mended yet? I ripped it under the arm the last time I wore it."

Joanna was sent to fetch the coat from a chest in the north chamber. The master had a considerable wardrobe, but it was in miserable condition. Buttons were missing, braid was loosened, and hems were torn. She found the blue coat. The sleeve stitching had given way, and the garment was badly wrinkled. She shook it out as best she could and took it downstairs.

The mending chore did little to improve Mistress Gifford's temper. She jabbed at the blue cloth with a needle threaded in brown. Didn't she know she should turn the coat inside out and work the seam that way? Joanna thought of showing her how, but checked herself. Small thanks she'd get for her pains, cross as the mistress was feeling.

Her dusting finished, she went to help Huldah with the midday meal. Hardly was it cleared away when the mistress called her.

"See if you can smooth some of the wrinkles out of this coat. It looks as if it had been slept in."

In the keeping room once more, Joanna stood irresolute. Should she go ahead as if she knew how to press the coat? The irons on the mantel seemed to wink at her balefully. How did one heat them? She'd better ask Huldah.

The older woman snorted at Joanna's ignorance but showed her how to go about the task. First an old blanket must be spread on the table. Over that went a sheet, worn but clean. The iron must be heated, just so, near the fire but not so near as to become sooty. At last the coat was spread out, a dampened cloth over it, and the iron in Joanna's hand. Gingerly she let it down upon the cloth; a cloud of steam arose. She slid the iron along to another spot, taking care, as Huldah had instructed, not to let it linger too long in any one place.

When she had finished, she held the coat up for Huldah's inspection.

"There's just one place." The older woman wrinkled her brow. "Here, on the cuff. I'll do it for you."

Joanna sighed. Of course Huldah would have to find some fault.

Huldah took a fresh iron from the fire, tested it with a wet forefinger, and started to press. "I can't be bothered with this cloth," she said, pulling it away. "I'll just set this down easy like and finish it."

A minute later she lifted the iron and stood back in dismay. Her touch had been less easy than intended. Clear on the cuff was the scorched imprint of the iron. Joanna would have cried out in vexation but for Huldah's shocked dismay.

"Oh Lordy, what have I done?" She rubbed in vain at the scorch with the wet cloth.

Joanna could feel herself shaking. She was the one who'd been told to press the coat. She would be held responsible. Whatever could she do? Desperately she picked up the coat and carried it to the window. The snow was letting up and the light growing brighter. Her misgiving deepened as she examined the burn. The cuff was ruined, and the coat as well, unless she could think of some way to repair it.

Slowly she turned the garment in her hands. On the inside a deep hem was turned under. Could she perhaps take enough cloth from it to patch the cuff? But a patch would never do. She would have to mend it so cleverly that no one would know it had been repaired. The task would not be easy. What if she should fail?

She recalled her mother sitting before the fire with her embroidery, saying softly to her father, "Joanna has a fine eye for colors. Look how she has separated the silks in this tangle. She can find three shades of rose where my eyes can see but one. And her stitches—how neatly they are laid on! She has a real talent for embroidery."

The firelight was the same, but the woman sitting next to it was not. "To think it should have been his *best* coat," Huldah was moaning.

"Have you a small needle and thread?" asked Joanna. "It should be a blue thread, and fine."

From a shelf Huldah took down a wooden box, extracted a needle and thimble and tangle of thread. But none of it was blue. Joanna examined the lining of the coat. Perhaps if she took out the stitches very carefully she could use the thread over again. And if that ran out, she could ravel out some of the silk of the fabric.

By midafternoon the cuff was mended as well as it ever would be. She had cut away the scorched portion of the material and fitted the piece from the hem in its place, tucking the edges under the braid trim so that only careful scrutiny would detect any alteration. For good measure she repaired the sleeve seam properly. Huldah stood over her. For once she could find no fault. She said as much and added, "You could have said 'twas me that burned it."

Joanna nodded. Hadn't she been sorely tempted? But it would not have made the coat whole again. "Accidents can happen to anyone," she said.

Mistress Gifford inspected the coat briefly. Her only comment was, "What a difference a good pressing makes. I can hardly see where I mended the sleeve now."

Joanna bit her lip. There was no point in saying she'd taken out the mistress's coarse brown stitches and set her own in their place. She had just returned to the keeping room when she heard the stamp of heavy boots in the shed. John Butt again, with more wood, she surmised.

A knock sounded on the door. That was strange. John usually walked straight in. Ruff gave a low growl, his fur bristling.

"See who it is," said Huldah, vigorously stirring the corncake for supper.

Joanna pulled open the door. Standing before her, brushing at the snow that clung to his breeches, his cheeks red with cold, stood Ross McCrae. For all that he drew his brows down over his eyes, he could not conceal a gleam of pleasure at the sight of her. But when he spoke his tone was impersonal and businesslike.

"I've brought a load of firewood," he said, "and I've a message for the Iron Master. The Widow Talbot has burned her hand and needs some woman to help her with the cooking and washing-up for a few days."

9

The Scots' House

"Burned her hand, eh?" said the Iron Master. "How bad is it?"

"Bad enough so she canna use it to lift things or even to prepare food."

"I see." Mr. Gifford paused. "Now who is there to send? Goody Pinnion? No, her husband is ailing again. Widow Page is abed with a fever, and Goody Webb's with child again and near her time. Not one can I bring to mind."

Huldah spoke. "What think you of sending Joanna?"

The Iron Master looked up in surprise. "I thought you needed Joanna here," he said.

"So I do," said Huldah, "but the Widow Talbot needs help more, with a burned hand."

"Very well, Joanna shall go." The Iron Master turned to Ross. "She'll be ready as soon as you've unloaded the wood."

Resentment rose in Joanna. Was she to have no say in the matter? Suppose she didn't want to help the Widow

Talbot? What was she, a chattel that was being lent around like a broom or a hoe among the settlers, depending upon which one had most need of her? She was about to open her mouth in protest when realization struck her. It made no difference how she might feel or what she might say. The Iron Master's word was law as far as she was concerned.

When Huldah urged, "Hasten and fetch your things," she sullenly obeyed. There was little to fetch—her night rail and a change of underclothing. As she was going out the door, her cloak over her shoulders, Huldah produced an enormous bearskin, its fur thick and glossy, with a faint musky scent. She put it into Joanna's arms with the admonition, "Wrap up tight."

The weight of the fur was surprising. Joanna nearly dropped it. But more amazing was the slight pat Huldah gave to her shoulder.

Minutes later Joanna perched beside Ross on the narrow seat of the sledge, wrapped from head to toe in the bearskin. The late-afternoon sun sparkled on the new-fallen snow, gilding the whitened branches of fir trees, brightening the blue of jays that scolded and darted about at their approach. Squirrels frolicked in high branches, their quick feet tossing down a powdering of snow. The sturdy horse drew the sledge with moderate gait, as if he were drawing his accustomed load of logs instead of two young people and a sack of meal. He blew great noisy breaths through his wide nostrils, shaking his head to jangle the metal parts of his harness.

Running alongside, barking imperiously, Ruff escorted them out of the yard and to the edge of the Iron Works. There he stood, one ear lifted, watching them out of sight.

"A fine dog, that," commented Ross. "My own Tam had a way of cocking one ear like that."

"Was he the same breed?"

"Nay, a collie, with a coat thick enough to keep out any snow or rain. Many's the night he kept me warm on the march down from Dunbar." He lapsed into a brooding silence.

The question she had half formed died on her lips. Ross's tone, the set of his mouth, warned her not to trespass. Perhaps some day he would tell her about the battle and more about his dog.

How quiet everything seemed. Snow covered the Iron Works, softening the outlines of the massive sheds. The water wheels stood motionless, icicles forming miniature frozen waterfalls on each descending arc. Only the stack of the vast furnace protruded from the smother, encircled by a rim of blackened, soot-stained snow.

" 'Tis downright eerie, without the din and the men about." Ross waved an arm at the buildings on the hillside. "I'd like well to get a look about some day, to learn how the iron is made. A body'd find much to admire midst all those machines." He turned his head for a last glimpse as they drove westward into woodland.

"It's just a great dark, smoky place with men and hammers making a frightful racket, enough to split your eardrums," said Joanna.

"Ye're daft, lass." Ross snorted. "Dinna ye ken that yon Iron Works is as fine as any in the whole world? 'Tis wondrous that such could be built here on the edge of the wilderness. 'Tis fair disheartening not to have so much as a peek inside the place."

"What's to prevent you? Mr. Gifford says that once the ice melts in the spring they'll start making iron again."

"What's to prevent me? 'Tis easy for you to ask, living next door to it all. But I'm stuck out in the woods more than a mile away, cutting wood. And by spring I may not—" His words dwindled. He left the sentence unfinished and clucked to the horse.

"I suppose people hereabouts do need a deal of wood to cook with and keep warm," offered Joanna equably.

"To keep warm!" Ross exploded. "I'm not cutting wood for houses, except some now and then for Mr. Gifford. There might be an end to that. I'm cutting it for the colliers to make into charcoal. Have ye any idea how much that takes?"

"How much?"

He drew a deep breath. "Enough to eat up a whole forest, and more too. It takes a vast amount of charcoal to melt the ore down."

So that was what the charcoal was for. Joanna had been ashamed to ask and display her ignorance.

The sun was lower now, its slanting rays giving but thin light and scant warmth. Joanna could feel her cheeks and nose tingling in the frosty air as the sledge moved steadily along the drifted road, between wood lots and open fields. She snuggled into the bearskin, grateful for the warmth of the shaggy fur.

"Was this bear shot nearby?" she asked.

"Likely it was," Ross said. "Anoka claims there are a good many in these very woods." He gestured at the forest ahead, its black branches like lace against the snow.

Under the heavy rug Joanna felt a shiver of apprehension. She couldn't help glancing among the trees on either side. But bears slept all winter, didn't they?

"Anoka," she asked, "who might he be?"

"An Indian who works with us, a good man with the ax. Duncan says savages take naturally to an ax and we'd better hang on to our scalps." He grinned.

Perhaps that was intended as some sort of grim joke— too grim for Joanna's taste. Suddenly she had to know more about what Ross had encountered in this new land. He'd certainly not been slaving in a kitchen.

"What is this Indian like? Are all the Scots cutting trees? Where do they all live? And who is the Widow Talbot?" Her questions rushed out in a torrent.

Ross threw back his head and laughed. "I canna for the life of me ken how so much curiosity is bundled up in one small package," he said, his eyes twinkling. "But I'll do my best to answer ye."

He and thirty others of the Scots were living in quarters the Iron Master had had built for them. The Widow Talbot got the meals and did the wash. Pleasant she was, and a good worker. Joanna pictured a gray-haired older woman, resembling Huldah, sunk in a chair beside the fire, cradling her injured hand.

Anoka, the Indian, was a Pequot brave no older than Ross himself—eighteen, that was—with muscles like steel cords. He'd narrowly escaped death at the hands of Connecticut settlers, and had fled to Massachusetts, where he'd been adopted by Poquanum, the biggest sachem in this area. He was a good worker when he felt like it, but some days he'd not show up at all—went hunting instead.

"Why does he work, if he's a chief's adopted son?" asked Joanna.

"For money," answered Ross briefly. "He gets paid two shillings a cord for cutting wood, and I think he must save it all. He has a leather pouch tied to his belt that's half full of coins. He's offered to take me hunting some day," he went on. "Small chance of that, though, with me tied to a woodpile." A glower settled upon his face.

Ross must hate being indentured as much as she. And he had an even longer term to serve—seven whole years. He too must have thought of running away.

The sled emerged into a clearing. Directly ahead, in the rosy light of the setting sun, stood a frame house, its unpainted clapboards still fresh and new, a faint glow shining in the windows.

"Oh, what a winsome place!" Joanna gasped in pleasure.

" 'Tis but rough within, far from as fine as the Iron Master's," warned Ross.

Fine it might not be, but the house had an air of cheer and friendliness, a sturdy strength that seemed to welcome her. The horse quickened his gait and turned into the yard.

A man emerged from the barn—a very giant of a man with snow clinging to his clothes, even to the cap pulled over his thatch of sandy hair. He looked familiar, but it was difficult to place these Scots without plaid or kilt. Ah, it was Duncan Muir. She remembered his towering form and rugged good humor even in the darkest days.

"Ross, me lad, I see ye've found a braw bonny lass for us." He hesitated a moment. Would he recognize her now, looking for all the world like a furry caterpillar in the bearskin? "Aye, 'tis no ither than the maid from the *Unity*. It's welcome ye air, Mistress Sprague."

To be called *mistress*, after a fortnight of being a kitchen wench! Joanna could have thrown her arms about him, snow and all.

"Come in, come in," he urged. "We'll let Ross put up the beast by himself."

Joanna felt herself lifted out of the sleigh and set down on a cleared space. Duncan headed toward the back door and put his hand on the latch to open it. Suddenly it swung wide, and a woman burst out. She was young and strongly built, with a mass of red-gold hair piled atop her head. In one hand she brandished a broom.

"Whisht ye, Duncan Muir. Off wi' yer boots now, ere ye come tromping up the floor."

"I'll have no female ordering me about," thundered Duncan. He bent over the woman and took the broom from her hand.

Joanna stepped back, aghast. What a sharp-tongued scold this woman was! Surely she was not the Widow Talbot. Could she be a neighbor come in to give a few hours' help? She half expected Duncan to take the woman over his knee and belabor her with the broom. Instead he was using it to brush the snow from his clothes. Then he attacked his boots, scraping off every vestige of ice.

"Be ye satisfied now?" he queried.

The woman stood with her hands on her hips, her head cocked to one side and—could it be?—a saucy smile on her face.

"That's some better," she admitted, her eyes dancing.

"To think we braw Scots must put up with a woman so fierce." When Duncan turned, Joanna could see that his face was split in a broad grin.

"Have ye the courage to come and meet the Widow Talbot, lass?"

The Widow Talbot? Joanna's picture of the gentle old lady shattered into bits. The gray hair, the resemblance to Huldah, the sorrowful fireside pose—all were dashed. This woman was no more than twenty-five, and about as much in need of help as a tigress. Then Joanna noticed the bandage tied about her right hand, and the lines of pain in her face.

"I'm Joanna Sprague." Was this her voice, so shy and uncertain?

"Maura's me name, as Irish as meself." The woman put her left arm about Joanna's shoulders, urging her into the house. "It's that glad I am to have another woman about," she said warmly. "I've been in sore need of another female to help me keep these Highland ruffians in their place."

They walked through a low shed into the kitchen. For a moment Joanna felt as if she had stepped into an inn, the room was so filled with men. Some sat on stools ranged about the walls, others on log benches on either side of a long trestle table. One lay on a low cot in a corner, his eyes closed, his scraggly gray beard limp upon the blanket. An orange cat lay on the hearth near a lanky man whittling a boat out of a stick of wood for two small boys whom Maura introduced as her sons, Hiram and Phineas. Hiram, dark and angular, was the older, about six. Phineas, a year younger, had round dark eyes and softly curling hair.

As Joanna stepped into the firelight, voices lifted, thick with a Scottish burr.

" 'Tis the lass from the ship."

"How's it farin' wi' ye?"

"Be ye well treated?"

The friendliness of their tone, their concern, warmed her more than the fire. It was as if they had opened their

ranks and welcomed her in. These men who'd lost home
and family and friends had understood what she had felt
at her father's death. And who knew better than they what
it was to face years of indenture?

Maura had picked up a wooden spoon in her left hand
and was clumsily stirring the contents of a large iron pot
hanging over the fire. Joanna noticed that she winced as
her bandaged hand came near the heat. She took the
spoon out of the widow's hand, drawing her away from
the hearth.

"You tell me what to do first," said Joanna, stirring the
pot. "Shall I wash the trenchers, or would you like me to
cut some slices of meat to broil? Or should I mix up some
corncake?"

Ross came in, seeming very youthful in the company of
the older men. When Joanna started to hack ineffectually
at the haunch of venison, he waved her away and cut neat
slices with apparently little effort. When she set a tub
on the table, he poured hot water and cold into it for
washing the trenchers and spoons. When she had mixed
a huge bowlful of cornmeal and milk with a bit of maple
syrup for sweetening, and looked in vain for pans like
Huldah's to bake the corncake, he fetched flat stones from
a pile in the shed and showed her how to set them near
the fire so the batter spread on them would bake to a rich
brown.

"I'd no idea ye'd such liking for kitchen work. And to
think we might've been eating good bannock these two
days past," said Duncan with a hearty laugh.

More than the heat of the fire made Ross flush. " 'Tis
just that I'm near starved," he said defensively. "If any of
the rest of ye had any spirit, ye'd lend a hand too."

The food disappeared with frightening swiftness, even the charred corners of corncake and the toughest pieces of meat, and the last smidgin of mush from the pot. Benches were pushed back; men sighed gustily in satisfaction. Duncan looked about the group, then turned to Ross.

"Can ye play us a tune, lad?" he asked. The room rustled with anticipation.

Ross dived into the shadows, returned with the bagpipes. He put the mouthpiece to his lips, tucked the bag under his arm, and began blowing air into it. With the three drone pipes uptilted over his left shoulder, he placed the fingers of both hands in careful precision on the chanter. A weird screeching wail arose as he adjusted the valves on the drones.

Ross took a stance in the middle of the room, his head thrown back, his gaze fixed on some distant, unseen place far beyond the farmhouse walls. The men pushed their stools and benches to the walls, leaving a cleared path through the room's center. Only the pulsing throb of the fire broke the waiting silence.

Then it came, a rushing torrent of sound. The skirling notes had a savage barbarity that tore at her heart. One minute they snarled with ferocity. The next they cried in a lament that held all the sorrow and tragedy of the world.

Joanna sat entranced, scarcely breathing. Beside her Maura held one boy in her lap; the other nestled at her feet. Ross paced back and forth, the music timed to his tread, his left arm pressing rhythmically against the sheepskin bag. Some of the Scots gazed at him and through him, as if hearing other pipers in other, far-off times. Some sat with their chins on their hands. And in the corner the

sick man, Davison, was frankly weeping, tears flowing
unheeded on his furrowed cheeks.

Duncan squared his massive shoulders. He seemed to
be returning from a great distance.

"Could ye not play something a bit less doleful?"

Ross quickened his pace. From the pipes came a warble
of hopping skirls and twists. Joanna could feel her pulse
quickening. Maura's foot was tap-tapping. The Scots were
nodding their heads in time to the music.

Maura stood up, letting the younger boy slide to the
floor. She held her full drab skirt with both hands, lifting
it above the rough boards. A few tentative steps she took,
quick and lively; then she was out in the open space, feet
flying, skirt twirling. A bright scarlet petticoat flounced
into view.

Around the walls the men began to clap their hands in
time to the tune. Duncan, after one moment of stunned
amazement, put one hand on his hip, the other behind
his head, and danced opposite Maura, improvising steps
to suit hers. As he danced, he sang in a strange, outlandish
tongue, his voice and the music of the pipes making the
room rock with sound.

Joanna found herself clapping her hands too, and singing the melody of the dance. The boys stood beside her,
drumming on her knees with their small fists. Merriment
so filled the room that it was some minutes before anyone took notice of the square, stern-visaged man who stood
in the doorway.

The newcomer's features were set in rectangular sever-
ity. Straight brows beetled over cold gray eyes. His nose
was long and thin. So was his mouth, over a squared-off
chin that jutted out in stormy indignation.

A voice said, "'Tis Obadiah Talbot," and Joanna recognized the man who had spoken against Wapaket outside the meetinghouse.

The mouthpiece dropped from Ross's lips. His fingers went slack on the chanter. Sound squealed from the drones in a snarl of wheezing sighs. Maura checked her twirl in swift panic. Stock still she stood, smoothing the gray skirt, twitching it to cover one exposed scallop of scarlet flannel. Her face as crimson as her petticoat, she waited for Goodman Talbot to speak.

The two little boys had as suddenly ceased their drumming on Joanna's knees. Now they pressed close to her, their small bodies tense.

"What manner of brawl is this?" Obadiah Talbot's voice was heavy with anger. "And did I see you, my own daughter-in-law, *dancing?*"

He could not have put more loathing into his enunciation of the word if he had been speaking of the most deadly of sins.

"And what's wrong with a bit of a jig?" inquired Duncan. Though he was a head taller than Goodman Talbot, even his booming voice seemed to have lost some of its confidence.

"'Tis the devil's own temptation! I'd thought you a sober man, immune to such folly, Duncan Muir." He turned to Maura. "This is the thanks I get for coming out on a winter's night to look in on the widow of my poor dead son John. I'd heard tell you were so laid up you had to call on Mr. Gifford for help." His eyes bored into her with dreadful accusation. "And I find you capering about like a loose woman!"

Joanna saw Maura recoil. "My hand is burned," she said.

"There's naught the matter with your feet," retorted her father-in-law venomously. He looked at Joanna. "Is this the bound girl from the Iron Master's house?"

How she hated to be termed thus. She bit off an angry retort, saying shortly, "Yes."

Goodman Talbot shook a finger in her face. "Beware of such abomination," he warned her, "lest ye fall into the pit of eternal fire."

Joanna shrank back, hating herself for her weakness, yet afraid of that menacing forefinger.

The man swung about. "I shall return to my quiet, godly home, and pray that you may turn from the wickedness of your ways." He gave one last scowl and went out the door.

A deep silence followed his departure. Ross squeezed the last breath of air from the bag, shook moisture from the mouthpiece. Clearly there'd be no more music, no more dancing this night—perhaps not any other night.

The men broke away in twos and threes, heading for the bedchambers above. Joanna tackled the dirty trenchers, scoured the iron pot. Maura led the boys to another room.

Duncan stood beside the fire, his huge frame towering. He looked at Ross. "There's ane thing to be thankful for," he said, "that we oursel's were born Scots, not gloomy preachin' killjoys like yon Puritan."

10

Maura

"John was no more like his father than milk is like brandy. He was as mild as his father is harsh."

Maura sat on a stool before the fire in the room she and her sons shared. On the first floor, it opened off the keeping room. Here she had brought her scant possessions. In one corner stood a four-poster bed. Nearby was the trundle bed, sagging under the weight of the two boys. A pine chest, a spinning wheel, some stools, and a table were the only other furniture.

Maura kept her voice low lest she disturb the boys. Opposite her, Joanna listened intently, sleep far from her thoughts. In her mind she could still hear the skirl of the pipes, feel the awesome hush that Obadiah Talbot had brought.

"John was a kind man." Maura looked into the fire, a half-smile curving her generous mouth. "Not once did he say a harsh word to me or to the boys."

"Where did you meet him?" asked Joanna. Had Maura's

been a case of love at first sight, the kind sung of in ballads?

"I don't know as you'd say we ever rightly met," said Maura. "He was always just there, the youngest of the Talbot boys, and the only one who treated me like a human being. To the others I was only the bondmaid, their servant for seven years."

Joanna sat bolt upright. "Were you indentured too?" she cried.

"That I was." Maura smiled ruefully. "Spirited away by a soul-driver when I was but ten years old. What manner of fiend is it that barters boys and girls? That one was all smiley about the mouth. 'Twasn't till later I saw the guile in his eyes. He'd a wee kitten in his pocket, showed it to me so friendly like. Said he'd give it to me for my own if I'd go with him. What child can resist a mewing bit of fur with blue eyes? I was after him in a trice."

"And then what?" Joanna could feel her heart pounding.

"The minute we'd stepped on board his ship, he clapped a hand over my mouth and carried me into the hold. There were others there, with eyes swelled shut from tears, but making not a sound, so fearful were they. I soon found out why. A whip can quick silence a child." She paused as if the memory were too painful to recall. "As soon as he'd kidnaped enough of us, he set sail for this colony, and in Boston he sold us to the highest bidders. Obadiah Talbot bought me."

What a bright, merry child Maura must have been! Joanna could picture her following the man along the wharf, her eyes alight with anticipation. And then to have been so betrayed!

"I was big and strong for my age," Maura went on, "and

soon I was doing most of the work around the house. Goody Talbot used to say she didn't know what she'd do when my term ended. I'd fancied going to Boston to work for wages and see a bit of life there. But John bespoke me, and his parents said 'twas my duty to marry him."

"Where did you learn to dance?" asked Joanna.

"In Ireland—where else? You don't think I'd have had the chance living with the Talbots." Maura sniffed derisively.

"Did you ever think of running away?" Joanna tried to keep her tone casual.

" 'Twas the only thing I thought about for months. I even talked about it with a boy bound out to another family. He tried, but got caught in Charlestown. When I saw what happened to him, I gave up the idea."

"Was he punished badly?"

"Set in the stocks and whipped, and had a year added to his indenture. I didn't fancy that. I'd had enough of whipping from Goody Talbot, and seven years seemed long enough without more."

"At least you got married and had children," said Joanna. "It must be wonderful to have a home of your own." What pure joy it would be to choose one's own curtains—yellow, perhaps—to hang at the windows, to have bowls of dried flowers on the tables, and a rug before the fire, with a shaggy dog lying on it.

"We never did have a house to ourselves," said Maura regretfully. "We stayed with John's folks. He being the youngest and the others all gone off, there was room enough. He'd just gotten a piece of land next to Adam Hawkes and was going to build us a house, when he was taken with the lung sickness and died."

The flames burned low with a murmuring sound. The cat curled at Maura's feet jumped into her lap, purring. She ran her hand over its orange fur.

"John's father said 'twas the will of God he should die," Maura continued, "though I've wondered if breathing in all that smoke and ash at the Iron Works might not have been more of a reason. John's mother said the Lord visited these afflictions on us to strengthen our faith. I was so near to losing mine I thought of drowning myself in the millpond. But there were the boys, God be thanked."

"How long have you been a widow? A month or two?" From the way Goodman Talbot had spoken, his son might have died last week.

" 'Twill be four years next month," said Maura. "And if you're wondering why I've not married again, 'tis because I'll not have any man telling me what bread I can or cannot put into my children's mouths. 'Twas bad enough having their grandfather watching every bite and be-grudging it." She gave Joanna a half-smile. "Besides, I'd not seen a man I could take a fancy to. So when Mr. Gifford offered me work here, I came gladly. Here I'm my own mistress, which I've never been before."

"How did you ever get away from the Talbots?"

"Half my wages go for a girl to help in the kitchen. I'm paying dear for my freedom, but 'tis worth every farthing."

Freedom? With thirty men to cook and scrub for? And two small boys to feed and clothe and raise?

Maura gave the cat a shove and stood up. It landed lightly, arched its back, and rubbed against her ankles. She walked softly to the trundle bed, regarding her sons tenderly. Hiram was sprawled over most of the bed, his thin arms stretched out above his head. Beside him Phineas was curled in a tidy cocoon. The cat jumped onto the bed and settled itself in the curve of Phineas's body.

Maura turned to Joanna. "I've talked more this night than I ought. 'Tis time for us to be getting to bed." She raised her hand and took the pins from her hair. It fell about her shoulders, a shining red-gold mantle.

"Where am I to sleep?" asked Joanna. Would the garret in this house be as cold as the Iron Master's?

"Here with me," rejoined Maura. She turned down the coverlet, disclosing snowy sheets laid over the billows of a feather bed. "You go in first on the inside," she said. "Then I can get up if Davison should call out."

In a few minutes Joanna had settled down in the heavenly warmth. A fragrance of lavender clung to the pillowcase. She burrowed her head into it and drifted off. Neither the howl of wolves nor the scream of a wildcat in the nearby forest disturbed her, not even the remembrance of Obadiah Talbot.

Days flew by swiftly, too speedily to suit Joanna. She worked hard and long, preparing kettles of stew and chowder, churning cream into butter, baking loaves of bread. There was the ailing Davison to tend, his eyes sinking deeper into his skull each day. The little boys, too, required attention. All day they tramped in and out of the house, seeking crumbs for the birds or apple parings for the squirrels.

Constant though the work was, it seemed far from arduous to Joanna. Here there was a freedom and tolerance not to be found in the Iron Master's house. Maura cared little whether Joanna swept the dirt into the fire or out the door; the main thing was to get it off the floor. In the matter of cooking she was equally unconcerned. No need to cut vegetables into precise cubes. Any size or shape would do. The Scots wouldn't care, Maura said with a chuckle, what the food looked like so long as there was enough of it.

Two cows and a score of chickens kept them in milk, butter, and eggs. Maura hoped for a few pigs to fatten up. And she wished there were sheep. She'd like well to have some wool to spin and knit up. The boys needed new socks. She felt downright slothful without some knitting or sewing at hand. Just as soon as her palm healed she must get some handwork under way.

Every night Joanna unwrapped the bandage and they both inspected the scabbed purple swath. It was taking long enough to heal, though it had happened quickly enough. The green pole supporting an iron pot had cracked in the intense heat of the fire and broken. Had Maura not been standing there and snatched at the handle, the pot would have fallen and its boiling contents poured over Phineas as he played on the hearth. What was a burned hand against a son's life?

The hand was healing well. Fortunately it had not festered. Every day brought a shrinking of the scabbed area and a widening of the tender new pink skin.

As the burn healed, Maura's spirits improved. She took to singing as she worked, confiding to Joanna that it made a body feel good to make a little music now and then. She'd never dared sound a note at the Talbots'. Joanna knew exactly how Maura felt. Hadn't she the same reticence at the Giffords'? Here she could talk, and talk she did. Soon she had told Maura about her own life, even of the time she and Debby had been rescued from the river by Yaweta.

"That Indian maid seems kind and gentle," said Maura. "I cannot fathom why folks hate her so."

Joanna beamed at her.

One afternoon Maura left Joanna in charge and went to visit the Talbots. That little she owed her mother-in-law, she said. Obadiah, she hoped, would be away on some errand.

The boys had played outdoors all morning and now were tired and restless. Joanna remembered a game that had amused her when she was younger. She peeled strips of birch bark off logs in the shed, smoothed them out, while the boys watched in keen anticipation. With a scrap of charcoal she drew on one the head of a deer, keeping it hidden from the boys. She folded the bark, turning the head under, and commanded Phineas, "You draw the neck and upper part of a body."

"A man or a woman?"

"Either one. Or a cat or a horse or a squirrel. Anything you like."

His eyes lit up. "Even a dog?"

She nodded in assent, her fingers busy with a bear's head for Hiram. "When you've each finished the top part of the body, fold the drawing under and exchange pieces of bark. But don't peek. That would spoil the fun," she admonished them.

While they scratched away, their faces screwed up in concentration, she went over to Tom Davison. He lay very still, his eyes fixed on some far-off point. She put her hand in his, her heart filled with grief that his long journey across the ocean would soon end in another, longer journey.

"Dinna sorrow for me, lass," he said, the words coming slowly and painfully. "I've had a good life. 'Tis the younger ones I grieve full sore about—like Ross, the seventh in his line to pipe. He'd have been at the right hand of the laird, like his father before him, had we not failed at Dunbar. Aye, the castle of Eildonan will be sad and silent without a McCrae to play the bagpipes. And the clan unco sorry with no piper to lead them to battle."

Joanna was longing to hear more, but Davison's words had grown so weak she had to bend over him to hear the last phrase. His hand lay limp on the blanket. The boys came near, holding out the birch bark, their eyes round in glee.

"What do we do now?"

Joanna pulled the covers up to Davison's chin, smoothed his thin hair, and said to him, "I'll be back in a bit." Then she led the prancing boys to the hearth.

"Now it's time for the feet," she said. "Trade drawings again."

A few minutes later they sat beside her, shrieking with glee. The bear's head was set on the forequarters of a dog bearing a strong resemblance to Ruff. The next section showed the lower part of a squirrel complete with furry tail, and below this protruded a pair of workman's sturdy boots. The deer's antlers topped a man's upper body over a bird's tailfeathers, with a horse's four feet underneath.

There had never been so funny a sight. The boys rolled over and over in the center of the room. Maura, coming in the door with a large sack in her arms, was startled. When, with upheavals of mirth, they showed her the cause, she beamed at Joanna. "I've not heard such good honest laughter since I left Ireland," she said. "It does me good to hear the boys so merry."

The sack was filled with wool from the Talbots' sheep. "I'm to spin it and will have half to keep for myself. 'Twill make fine stockings for the boys, and perchance a new pair for myself." She looked critically at her much-mended hose. "Of course it's to be washed and combed and carded before it can be spun. If ye can help with the washing, I can do the rest, even with this hand."

Under Maura's direction, Joanna plunged the greasy, matted wool into warm soapy water. When dry, the wool was fluffy and far lighter in color than before. The whitest parts of the fleece Maura set aside for dyeing. "I could make it yellow," she mused. "Onion skins make a bright gold. Or I could use bark for a brown. Or I could even"— she hesitated—"dye it red."

"Like your petticoat?" asked Joanna.

Maura's blush rose to the roots of her hair. " 'Twas wicked of me to spend good money on such. But I'd just got my first pay when the peddler knocked on the door. He spread out his things, and when I saw the red dye I knew I must have it. Ever since I was a wee thing I longed for a red petticoat like my mother's. So I bought the dye and colored my old one as scarlet as hers."

"You weren't wicked. It was your money, wasn't it?" Joanna couldn't let Maura inflict blame on herself for such a trifle as a pack of red dye.

"There's a bit left," Maura said. "Ye may have it if ye wish."

"Thank you, but I don't know that I'd ever have a chance to use it."

After the washing, the wool had to be combed. One sunny afternoon Maura showed Joanna how to take two boards studded with short nails and draw them in opposite directions over a handful of the wool until all the fibers were going one way. The operation took patience. More than that, it took skill. Maura seemed to have a knack for the task. Joanna was sure each tuft of wool knew that when it came beneath Maura's hands it had better obey. She was just as sure that the wool knew when the Giffords' bondmaid was handling it, and acted accordingly.

" 'Tis no wonder I can comb," said Maura. "I've been doing it since I was that high." With one arm she indicated a small child's height. "Hiram, come here and see what ye can do with these," she invited. "You too, Phineas. I was no older than you when I began."

Reluctantly the boys drew near. "We were going out to play in the snow," objected Hiram, his dark eyes twinkling.

Phineas took up the boards, tentatively drew them across the wool, lifting, pulling, straightening. Joanna looked on in amazement. Maura smiled approvingly. "He has my hands," she said. "He's that deft he can do anything."

Maura touched the curls of fluffy wool, flexing the fingers of her injured hand. "I believe I could spin a bit," she said. "I'm that eager to begin, and 'twould not hurt the palm."

Joanna brought the spinning wheel into the light. Maura gave the wheel a turn with her hand, tightened the hempen cord that encircled the rim of the wheel, and fastened a bit of the wool to the spindle.

"Now," she said, "this is the way it goes." She touched

the wheel lightly, pulled the wool out between thumb and forefinger, drawing it out gently as the whirring spindle twisted it. A fine thread of yarn appeared as if by magic.

They became so engrossed in the project that, before any of them realized it was growing late, the light had faded and the Scots trooped in the door, stamping their feet and sniffing hungrily.

"May the Lord help me!" exclaimed Maura. "I clear forgot to make the bread for tomorrow."

11

The Indian Village

Noon of the next day saw Joanna tramping through the snowy woods, carrying a sack of bread and cheese for the men's lunch. She'd have no trouble finding them. Their footsteps had worn an icy path through the snow.

Out here in the clear frosty air she couldn't help feeling lighthearted. There was an invigorating, bracing quality in the cold that gave wings to her heels. Despite the heavy sack, she sped quickly along.

Soon she heard the ringing of axes on tree trunks, the staccato blows making a curious unrhythmic melody. Then she came within sight of a clearing where logs were piled in corded lots and brush was heaped in an untidy mass. She had taken a few paces into the woods on the other side when a voice cried out sharply, "Stop where you are!"

Mystified, she obeyed. There came a crackling of branches, a rush of air, and a thundering crash. The earth shook. Not ten feet from where she stood a tree lay on the ground, quivering from the force of impact. Ross climbed over the trunk and fought his way through a thicket of limbs to her side.

"You're no' hurt?"

She was trembling. What if he had not called out? She managed a smile. "I'm glad you warned me."

His face was fiery red, whether from the exertion of chopping or anxiety over her she could not tell. He swallowed hard and pushed a lock of dark hair back from his forehead.

"'Tis no place for a woman here in the forest. Ye'd best be getting back to the house, where ye'll be safe."

Was this all the welcome he could muster? Very well, she knew when she was not wanted. She thrust the sack into his hands.

"Here," she said briefly. "I'd no intent to get in your way."

He threw her an exasperated glance. "'Tis not that, lass, so much as other dangers. There still be wolves about. And Indians."

Indians. One instant Ross stood alone, facing her. The next moment a lithe form appeared beside him. The dark skin glowed with a ruddy fire. Even in woodsman's clothing the youth had a savage, untamed air. Could it be because of the single feather twisted in his straight black hair? Joanna recognized him then. This was the young brave who had spoken with Yaweta after the Sabbath-day service. He must be Ross's friend too.

"Anoka." Ross turned in pleasure. "This is Joanna."

The Indian regarded her inscrutably.

"I am a friend of Yaweta's," ventured Joanna. Did a faint friendliness light the dark eyes? It was hard to tell.

"You go to house now," he said. The words came slowly but unmistakably clear.

" 'Tis what I but told her," agreed Ross.

If that was the way they felt, she'd certainly not stay a moment longer. She whirled and, without saying good-by, picked up her skirts and broke into a swift run. As she crossed the clearing, Ross called out, "Wait, Joanna, I didna mean—"

But she did not slacken her pace. They'd made it clear enough she wasn't wanted. She was within sight of the house when she saw a crimson-cloaked figure coming along the road from Hammersmith. As the distance between them lessened, Joanna recognized her. In happy surprise she waved and called, "Yaweta!"

Minutes later she urged the Indian girl into the house, introduced her to Maura, and sat her down at the table. Over hot soup and bread Yaweta explained that she was on her way to the Indian village. Once a month she was allowed to go to see her mother.

Joanna nearly choked on her soup. She had supposed Yaweta's mother was dead. To cover her amazement she asked, "What is an Indian house like?"

Yaweta set her bowl down on the table. "You come with me, see for yourself."

Joanna looked at Maura. How she would like to see how the Indians lived!

"You should be safe with Yaweta," said Maura hesitantly. "I can get along without you for a few hours. The boys will be here to help me." She smiled at the two tousled heads.

"Will you tell us about the Indian village?" asked Hiram. "Do they really hang up scalps in their houses?"

"And eat dogs?" inquired Phineas with burning intensity.

"Shush." Maura gave each young shoulder a shake.

Half an hour later Joanna and Yaweta were deep in the forest. Yaweta led the way, following a narrow path worn by moccasined feet. The terrain was rough and hilly, broken by occasional huge boulders and jutting ledges of granite. Twice they picked their way through swampy lowlands. How far was it? Joanna wondered. Three miles? Four?

She had begun to tire when Yaweta stopped at the rim of a hill. At one side lay a fresh mound of earth, on which were placed two carved wooden bowls containing dried corn and berries, three small baskets, a bow and arrow, and a tomahawk. Joanna would have picked up one of the bowls had not Yaweta restrained her.

"It is a grave," she said solemnly. "The food and weapons are for the spirit of the warrior on his journey after death."

Joanna stepped back, awed and a little frightened.

"There is the village." Yaweta pointed to a cleared hollow beside a creek. A dozen low huts were scattered about, smoke rising from their roofs. Children played in the open space. Three dogs, seeing the girls, ran toward them with menacing gait. Lean and scruffy, they barked hoarsely. Joanna stood still, holding out one hand for the animals to sniff. She'd done the same dozens of times with strange dogs, and every time she'd ended up stroking their heads.

These dogs were different. One jumped for Joanna's wrist, caught it in fierce teeth. Had Yaweta not kicked at the beast, its bite would have broken the skin. She spoke sharply in a strange tongue. The dogs slunk off, tails down, turning now and then to give an angry snarl.

Joanna rubbed at the blue spots where the animal's teeth had gripped her wrist. She looked at the huts. The children had evidently alerted the occupants, for several squaws emerged from skin-covered doorways to peer at the newcomers.

One woman broke away from the group and came to embrace Yaweta. Beneath her evident joy at seeing her daughter, the woman had an air of dejection. Dark hair, bound at the temples by a piece of leather, lay limp about her shoulders. Her deerskin dress hung carelessly, devoid of ornament. The other women, by contrast, wore colorful headbands and clothing adorned with pieces of polished shells. They gathered about Joanna, fingering her hair, examining her cloak, exclaiming at her fair skin. One took Joanna's cheek between her thumb and forefinger and pinched it sharply.

Joanna jerked away and followed Yaweta and her mother into one of the huts. A small fire in the center gave off a little light. Some of the smoke escaped through a hole in the roof; the rest eddied about the interior. Skins of wild animals lay on pole frameworks at the sides of the hut. Wooden bowls and reed baskets made up the rest of the furnishings. In one corner sat an aged man, wrinkled as a walnut, swaying back and forth. At sight of Yaweta he wheezed a few words, then lapsed into silence.

"My grandfather," Yaweta explained. "This is his house."

Yaweta's mother made gestures to Joanna to be seated on one of the couchlike structures. As she sat down, a mouse ran out from under it and darted outside through a crevice. Joanna started violently, but no one else paid any attention. Evidently the mouse was an accepted member of the household.

From a basket Yaweta's mother produced a mixture that resembled coarse meal. She handed a gourdful of it to Joanna, then to Yaweta. Joanna took some and tasted it gingerly. For all it looked like mud and flies, it had a pleasant taste. She pointed to her mouth and smiled at the mother.

"It is dried corn and berries," said Yaweta. "She is pleased that you like it."

Joanna settled back. Now that she was accustomed to the smoke, she could almost enjoy herself. She picked up a wooden bowl. How cleverly it was carved, following the grain of the wood. The bowl was as smooth as satin. There was even a handle, with the head of a fox carved upon it.

From the smoky ceiling hung a few long tufts of hair, held together at one end by what appeared to be a bit of leather. Some of the hair was dark, some was light, and one tuft, definitely reddish. Suddenly, with ghastly clarity, Joanna knew what they were. Scalps! Hadn't Hiram warned her?

The deerskin flap hanging in the doorway was thrust aside, and a woman entered, stout and elaborately dressed, with red ribbons braided in her hair.

"The new wife of my grandfather," explained Yaweta.

With an air of arrogance, the woman brushed past Joanna, spoke curtly to Yaweta and her mother, and placed beside the fire a large piece of meat. From it she hacked a generous slice, which she proceeded to broil over the fire.

The meat sent up a savory odor. Joanna could feel her

mouth watering. She'd had a long walk and was keenly
hungry. How good the meat would taste!

When the slice had cooked to a crispy brown, the
woman let it cool briefly, then took it in both hands and
began to devour it. Joanna looked on in amazement, but
Yaweta and her mother paid no heed. Joanna set her jaw.
She probably wouldn't have relished the meat anyway.
Perhaps, as Phineas had said, the Indians did eat dogs.
The thought was enough to drive away any appetite she
might have had.

Soon Yaweta arose, bade her mother good-by, and led
Joanna from the hut. At the crest of the hill the girls
paused to look down at the village. Beside the doorway
stood Yaweta's mother, a lonely figure, with one hand
raised in farewell.

The way back seemed longer. The girls traveled silently,
their feet making little sound in the soft snow. They had
covered perhaps half the distance when Yaweta slowed to
a stop and pulled Joanna off the path behind a large
boulder. A finger to her lips, she peered around the side of
the rock, then motioned to Joanna to do the same.

From their hiding place the girls could see a clear space
ahead where one trail crossed another. While they
watched, Wapaket, clad in his white man's finery, came
from one direction. From the other came a group of young
Indian braves in deerskin leggings and shirts bedizened
with feathers and shells. With savage whoops they surrounded the older man.

Joanna could feel her heart thumping. Were they going
to kill Wapaket, even scalp him before her eyes? Too
frightened to move, she stood transfixed. She could feel
Yaweta's hand trembling on her arm.

The circle widened. One brave approached Wapaket, his right arm stiffly extended. He swung it in a wide arc and brought the flat of his palm against the Indian's cheek. There was a loud slap as his hand met flesh.

Wapaket had a knife in his belt. Would he use it to defend himself? She'd heard that Indians were very proud, would brook no insult. To her utter mystification, Wapaket stiffened but made no move. His hands hung motionless at his sides.

The brave swung his left arm in the same fashion. His palm met Wapaket's other cheek with a resounding thwack. There were five young warriors in the group. One by one they stepped up to Wapaket and administered the same treatment to a burst of savage jeers—left cheek, right cheek, slap, thwack. Joanna could feel her own head jerking back as blow followed blow.

At length the cruel show was over. The braves went one way, howling fiendishly, and Wapaket slowly stumbled in the opposite direction, mumbling to himself.

When Yaweta finally signified that it would be safe to go on, the girls proceeded fearfully. To Joanna each bush, each ledge, seemed to conceal a wild savage who might leap out upon them. Now she could understand why Ross and Anoka had urged her to return to the house. They had doubtless seen the Indian band earlier in the day.

Yaweta slowed her pace. "I am much troubled," she said. "I know the white man's God is good, and I wish to be a Christian. But my father is a Christian and he suffers much. He once told the Indians that if a man strike them on one cheek, they should turn the other. The young men do not think of what it really means. They take much amusement in making my father turn his other cheek."

So that was why the braves had struck Wapaket.

"White men told my father it is not good to have more than one wife. So my father cast off my mother because she was not the first wife he had taken. She had to return to my grandfather's house in disgrace. My grandmother is dead, and my grandfather's new wife does not like my mother. She must do all the hard work. Sometimes she does not have enough to eat."

Yaweta looked at Joanna, her eyes deep pools of grief. "She might starve if Anoka did not take food to her."

"Is Anoka your brother?" asked Joanna.

"He was to be my husband," said Yaweta simply. "Long ago it was arranged by our fathers. But now my father says I must marry a Christian, and I must obey my father." Her face was tragic. She threw Joanna an appealing look. "I need a friend to talk with, someone who can understand what is here." She put a hand on her heart.

12

Lament for a Scot

Dusk had fallen by the time Joanna reached the house. Maura met her at the door, her face sad. At either side the boys clutched at her skirt, their eyes wide. As Joanna stepped inside, she could sense the stillness.

Instinctively she looked toward the bed in the corner. The sheet was drawn up over the pillow. Beneath it showed the dim outline of Davison's head.

"He's gone," said Maura softly. "I thought he was just lying there with his eyes closed as he often did. But when I went to him I saw he'd stopped breathing." She shook her head sorrowfully. "'Twill be hard on the others."

But the Scots had seen so much of death, and Davison had been near it for so long that they accepted the news with stoic demeanor. Ross was sent to inform the Iron Master and to find out what arrangements would be made for the burial. He returned later in the evening with a length of cloth to be used as a winding sheet, and word that Davison would be buried in the northeast corner of the graveyard. If the grave was to be ready for to-morrow, they'd need to work in shifts through the night, for the frozen ground would be difficult to dig. They might have to build fires to thaw it.

The men drew lots to see who would commence work in the graveyard, and a few followed Ross to the designated plot. Some went off to catch what rest they might, and others went to the barn. Soon there came a sound of sawing and hammering. Fortunately there'd been boards enough stored in the barn for a coffin.

Wearily Maura and Joanna went to bed. Though fatigued by hours of walking in the open air, Joanna could not sleep. In her mind she went over again her visit to the Indian village. How sad for Yaweta's mother to lose husband and child because of Wapaket's conversion to Christianity! Why should religion bring about so much sorrow and dissension? It was the cause of the present trouble in England, where people like her parents who had loved the Church, with its traditions and ceremonies, its candlelight and gleaming altar, were hunted and hated by those who considered such symbols trappings of papacy. Men of the Puritan armies had broken the statues in churches, whitewashed over ancient paintings, and smashed stained-glass windows. Some had used chapels as stables for their horses.

It was hard to associate someone like Mr. Whiting with Oliver Cromwell, so fiercely dedicated to stamping out what he considered sin and sinners. Mr. Whiting seemed gentle and kind. One felt that he would go out of his way to keep people from doing wrong, would even forgive them their past offenses. And Mistress Whiting—she might belong to the same sect as Cromwell, but she was imbued with love and charity.

Poor Wapaket! Once he must have worshiped Indian gods. Did he not fear their wrath for forsaking them? Torn between two faiths, the old superstitions of his people and the commandments of the white man, could he find comfort in the teachings of Christianity?

And Yaweta. How confused she must be in her present plight! Joanna tried to imagine herself in such a situation. Suppose her father had given her to the Indians to raise, and had sent her mother to live as an unwanted poor relation somewhere? Wouldn't it be natural to hate the religion that had brought about such disaster? Yaweta must have a very forgiving nature to be trying to understand the Bible when its teachings had wrought such havoc in her family life.

At length Joanna fell into a troubled sleep. In her dreams she was once more in the Indian hut, but not as a visitor. The stout, greedy Indian matron shouted at her, hit her about the face and arms, and ordered her to go outside and search for nuts under the snow.

When morning came, a weary, subdued group of Scots ate their breakfast. Today they wore their kilts and plaids, seeming to stand taller, with an air of pride. Joanna overheard Duncan say, "'Tis glad I am to get out of those galligaskins," as he slapped at his kilt, and she knew he was referring to his workaday breeches.

When the meal was over, Maura bundled up Hiram and Phineas. "Will you be taking them to the Talbots'?" asked Joanna.

"No, they'll come with us. They're not too young to

know what death is. When it strikes close to them they'll not fear it as much as if it were strange to them."

Ross appeared, the bagpipes tucked under his left arm. Joanna and Maura donned cloaks and woolen hoods and led the boys outside. On a low sled that had been part of the night's work lay the coffin. Ross took his place at the head of the line. Behind him marched Duncan and another man, each holding a hempen rope attached to the sled. Behind the coffin walked two other Scots, also holding ropes. Then came the remaining Scots, two by two. At the very last walked Maura and Joanna, each with a boy by the hand.

While they formed the line, Ross had been tuning up on the pipes. At a word from Duncan, he set off, with a burst of plaintive sound. The wailing notes sounded across the snowy fields with a savage sorrow, echoing back from ledge and forest in a tragic lament.

The rough track to the meetinghouse and burying ground led up hills and down into swampy lowlands. The men walking at the back of the sled had as much work to keep it from sliding downhill as had those at the front to pull it up the inclines.

Joanna felt tears starting to her eyes. She was not crying for Davison alone. The music of the bagpipes, the sight of the marching men in travel-stained kilts and plaids, stirred new emotions within her. She felt that she was mourning all men who had gone to their deaths in battle or on foreign shores. She glanced at Maura, saw that her cheeks too were wet.

" 'Tis the pipes, and the men marching," said Maura, brushing away her tears. "They fair stir a body."

Mr. Whiting was waiting for them at the open grave.

With him were Mr. Gifford and the Scots who'd been billeted in village homes. As at her father's burial, there were no prayers and no sermon. After the coffin had been lowered into the grave in complete silence and covered over, Mr. Whiting expressed sympathy to Duncan as the leader of the Scots. Later he spoke to Ross.

"You play the bagpipes handsomely," he said. "I'd like to know more about your Scottish music. Do you play other airs, marches and such?"

"Aye," replied Ross briefly.

"His piping's that lively 'twould make the dead march," offered Duncan. He cast a hasty glance at the freshly covered grave. "Not that I'm referring to Davison, God bless him. 'Tis just a saying," he finished guiltily.

Mr. Gifford approached Maura. "How is your hand?" he asked.

"Much better, sir," she replied, bobbing him a curtsy.

"How soon do you think you can get along by yourself again?"

"In a day or two, I'm sure."

A day or two. Joanna's heart sank. How could she go back to the gloomy, stiff Gifford household after the easy warmth of the Scots' house?

"Joanna's been a wondrous help to me," Maura was continuing. "I'd like it well could she come again in the spring when it's time to make soap."

Return in the spring! What a happy prospect.

"Let me know when you have need of her." Mr. Gifford turned to Joanna. "We'll expect you the day after to-morrow."

The return to the Scots' house was no formal procession. Chilled from standing about the grave, the men moved quickly in small knots of two or three. Hiram and Phineas were stumbling along the rough track, well out of sight of the graveyard, when Duncan came up behind them, dragging the sled.

"Would ye mind?" he asked Maura. In strong arms he lifted Phineas and set him down on the planks nailed to the wooden runners. "Now you, Hiram." The second boy settled into place.

"Giddap!" shouted Phineas joyfully, heedless of the use to which the sled had been put a short time earlier. To Joanna's surprise, Duncan neighed and pranced, for all the world like a fiery steed instead of the tired, grieving man he had been a few minutes before.

Maura looked at them sagely. " 'Tis the way of the world. There's no use in grieving over what's gone. We might as well make use of what's left to us. And there's nothing like children to ease sorrow."

Back at the house, the men changed quickly into work clothes. Trees must be felled, wood cut into lengths, regardless of the fact that one of their number had died. When they had gone, Maura invited Joanna, "Would ye like to come with me whilst we take a closer look at those plaids? I durst not peer at them too closely before, but they seemed to me sore dirty and downright odorous. I wonder now, could we not wash and mend them?"

Clearly the plaids were in need of attention. For four months they'd been cloak and coverlet to the Scots. Dull, dirt-encrusted, stiff with grime, they had an odor that was far from pleasant.

For most of the afternoon Joanna drew water, heated it, and soused the woolen lengths in soapy baths. Together she and Maura stretched hemp on pegs from wall to wall in every room and spread the dripping wools to dry. How bright the colors were! How handsome, how bold the combinations of green on dark blue, with gold and scarlet lines meeting in colorful squares! The rooms seemed hung about with brilliant banners.

The next day Joanna spent mending the plaids. Every available minute she plied her needle, reweaving rents, catching together tears, darning holes. She had no trouble recognizing Ross's tartan. Why was his plaid so worn and obviously older than the others? It didn't make sense. He was younger than the rest. His plaid should have been newer. She had all she could do to mend it decently. It was so threadbare it would not hold together much longer.

That evening Ross helped as usual, filling the water hogshead, bringing in fresh wood, even lifting the heavy pot of stew off the fire for her. When her chores were finished and she had settled herself before the fire, she took up his plaid again to reweave a place where the threads had worn cobweb-thin.

"Dinna waste yer time on it, lass," he said. " 'Tis unco worn."

"How did it get in such a state?" she asked. "I'd heard a plaid would last a lifetime."

"And so that one did." He traced the line of red with his finger. "It was my father's."

"Oh?" Joanna turned a questioning gaze upon him.

"After I found him that day"—his voice broke on the words—"I wrapped him in my plaid. 'Twas new and strong and would keep out the cold and wet. I took his plaid and his pipes." He looked into the fire, a faraway light in his eyes, as if he were seeing there more than the flickering flames.

One by one the Scots drifted off to bed. Duncan went out to the barn to see that the doors were shut fast. Wolves had killed three pigs on the next farm only two nights ago.

For a few minutes Ross and Joanna were alone. The fire had burned down to a pulsating glow that gave off an even throb of sound. Ross picked up the bagpipes and paced up and down restlessly, softly playing a melancholy air.

"The lament this afternoon was not for Davison alone," he said. " 'Twas for your father and mine, as well."

On the verge of tears, she answered, "I thought it might be." A gloomy silence fell. It weighed upon her heart. She must try to bring Ross back from the doleful past.

"Are the bagpipes hard to play?" she asked. He was a piper born and bred. Perchance if he talked of piping he'd be less sorrowful.

" 'Tis not verra difficult," he said. "Here, stand up and I'll show ye."

He brought the instrument to her, tucked the sheepskin bag under her elbow, placed her fingers on the chanter, and put the mouthpiece to her lips.

"Now," he said, "ye squeeze the bag, thus, to send air into the pipes. And ye blow air into the bag to keep the pressure right. Gie it a try. But dinna attempt to blow and squeeze at the same time."

The bag felt like a pillow under her arm. She pressed it and moved her fingers on the chanter. No sound came forth. Ross gave her elbow a sharp push against the bag. A series of eerie squawks arose. She almost dropped the instrument.

Ross laughed. "Try it again. And place your fingers so."

This time the sound was not so raucous. And the next, it sounded almost like a chord played by Ross.

Loud thumps sounded from the floor above. A voice called down, "Can a mon get nae sleep?"

Joanna looked guiltily at Ross. He shrugged his shoulders and said, "We'll gie it anither try when 'tis no so late."

She handed him the instrument. As he took it, he said, "Would ye keep the pipes safe for me, lass, when I gang awa'?" His tone was deep with urgency.

"I don't understand," she faltered.

"The first chance that comes, I'll be leaving here. I canna bear to be bound this way."

So he was planning to run away. She had guessed it that day when he had brought her to this house. Surely he must know the penalty, the public flogging and the added year of indenture. And should he make good his getaway, there were the dangers of the wilderness winter.

She had opened her mouth to warn him, to beg him not to go, when the door burst open and Duncan came in, stamped snow from his boots, and settled down by the fire, saying, "Any wolves that get into the barn this nicht would need the de'il's own help."

She waited a few moments longer, hoping for a word alone with Ross. It was no use. She'd have to wait for another time and hope that before Ross set off he'd listen to her.

13

Spring at the Iron Works

Although for months snow and ice blocked the roads and river, nearly isolating Hammersmith from other towns, there was no lack of neighborly visiting within the village.

With the Iron Works shut down, many men went into the forest to cut wood or cord it, glad for a few shillings to compensate in part for lost wages. Some worked on wooden molds for the casting of hollow ware. Others made handles for tools, helves for axes and hammers.

What with cooking and mending and cleaning, women's work was never done. But in the winter, with the men sometimes at home to look after the children, the women could get out for a bit and visit with neighbors.

Often a tap came on the Giffords' back door in mid-afternoon when one or more of the Hammersmith women who had known Huldah for several years came to call. Some brought evidence of their skill—a new quilt pattern, an intricate knitting stitch, or a candle made from the waxy bayberries that grew by the shore. Others sought Huldah's aid in culinary problems. How did she get her corncake to cook through without drying out? Did she always use onions in her venison stew? Had she any luck in making jelly from the wild grapes? And those red berries that grew close to the ground—was honey the best sweetening for them?

Joanna found herself gradually slipping into the life of the village. Now and then she was sent to the company store for an ell of linen to make into towels. Or for salt, or sugar, pins, or shoelaces. The store was a fascinating place, filled with hogsheads, boxes, and bales containing household goods and staples. Calico, buttons, stockings, spades, tobacco, knives, paper, and even ribbons were there.

Christmas came and went without freedom from daily tasks and without feasting or caroling, for the Puritans frowned upon such pagan celebration. A woman in Salem was fined five shillings for serving plum pudding and wassail, it was said. Recalling other Christmases, with singing and merriment, sweetmeats and a roasted goose, Joanna felt more than a twinge of regret.

Just as she had begun to think that the winter would never end, spring came in a rush. She awakened one day to the sound of rain dropping gently on the roof. All morning it dripped from the eaves, forming a watery curtain across the windows. By afternoon the rain thinned to a mist, and from the rapidly melting snow rose a thick vapor. For two days the world was wrapped in a vast cloud that blurred sound and sight.

The third day the sun shone on a new-washed landscape. Only a few scattered patches of snow remained in the deeper hollows. Brooks were filled to overflowing, and the Saugus River was a swollen torrent.

As one day followed another, the Iron Works came to life, like a slumbering giant that awakened, yawned, and stretched first one and then another limb until its whole body was in motion. The canal must be cleared of all debris. The flood gates at the dam must be lowered, lest rising waters of the pond flood Adam Hawkes's land. More than once his good pastures and planting fields had been ruined by water backed up behind the dam. The wooden sluices had to be checked and repaired where ice and snow had sprung some of the seams.

Stonemasons repaired the walls of the huge water wheels, taking special care with the one beside the great furnace. Should any water leak through and penetrate to the crucible, the instant vaporization of moisture would create an explosion that would wreck the furnace and kill or maim any workmen nearby.

The great furnace was cleared of all slag. The egg-shaped cavity where the charcoal, ore, and flux combined in fiery magic to make molten iron must have its boshes and lining scraped clean. Supplies of raw materials must be checked to ensure a supply sufficient to keep the furnace in operation once it started to blow. A fire was kindled in the furnace and kept burning for three days to make sure all moisture was driven out.

At last all was in readiness. Mistress Gifford, Joanna, and Debby joined with wives and children of the ironworkers to witness the starting-up of the furnace.

A parade of loaders marched from the supply sheds on the top of the hill across the bridge over the water wheel to the platform beside the giant stack. Mr. Gifford himself checked off the first loading—scores of baskets of charcoal, then barrows of ore and gabbro, emptied layer upon layer onto the flaming fire in the bottom of the furnace.

The great water wheel turned. The giant bellows wheezed and blew a blast of air into the burning mixture. Sparks flew up, and a cloud of red smoke arose. The women and children stepped back, brushing sparks from their clothing, their eyes smarting from the smoke. One young wife cried out, "Oh, my wash! 'Twill be covered with soot!" And she ran to rescue her morning's work.

A few days later, Joanna was drawing water from the well when a wagon lumbered into view from the woods lying to the westward. Something about the driver's looks caught her eye. A moment more, and she recognized Ross. As he drew nearer, she saw the wagon was filled with charcoal, and Ross was as black as the charcoal itself. His hands and face were covered with soot; even his clothes were impregnated with black dust.

She ran over to the road where he must pass. "So you're a collier now," she greeted him. "Do you like it better than woodcutting?"

He ran a blackened finger inside his shirt collar, and shrugged his shoulders. " 'Tis a deal dirtier," he said, "but it takes real skill to turn sticks of wood into good-quality charcoal. Nearly a fortnight's tending went into this load, and not much sleep for anyone." His eyes looked tired and bloodshot.

"Would you like a drink of good fresh water from the well?"

He smiled. " 'Twould be welcome. I'm that thirsty. But first I must deliver this load and get a receipt for it."

Half an hour later he walked hesitantly into the yard. Joanna met him with a gourd of water and a piece of plum cake. He accepted them with thanks and drank the water in long, deep swallows. The cake he munched on appreciatively while regarding the furnace's fiery glow and its procession of men pouring load after load into the smoky maw.

"Could I but see the works from the inside," he said earnestly. "I'd like well to learn how the ore is smelted and the bars worked into rods."

"What about your plan to—" began Joanna, then stopped. Debby was drawing near, her ears sharp as a fox's. She was nearly dancing with excitement.

"Come into the barn," she cried to Joanna. "John Butt's dog has new puppies."

"Pups, eh?" Ross was after her in an instant. Joanna hurried to follow. In a dark corner of the hay they found the dog wearily nursing five small bundles of black and white. She growled menacingly at their approach.

"Best leave her alone," said Ross. "'Twould only upset her to go nearer." He spoke to Debby then. "You're big enough to get her a bowl of milk. In a day or two she may let you pick up one of the puppies."

Debby ran to get the milk. They followed her into the sunlight.

"I'd like well to take one of those pups to Hiram and Phineas," said Ross. "Phineas is near eatin' his heart out for a dog. He has a pet squirrel he keeps in a wee cage till it be grown enow to fend for itsel'. Can ye imagine a lad wi'out a dog?" His glance made it clear such a situation was unthinkable.

"Did you always have a dog?" asked Joanna.

"Ofttimes two or three. But Tam was the best of the lot. After the battle 'twas he found my father's body. All through the march he'd seek me out at night and sleep beside me. Even during the week we lay sick in Durham, he kept watch outside the cathedral and was waiting for me when we set out for London." His eyes were warm with the memory.

"And when you took ship?"

"He was on the dock. I'd like well to know what became of him. 'Tis not unlikely he found his way back to Eildonan."

"I suppose that's where you'll go when your term is up," she said.

"When my term is up? I'll not stay here seven years, sweating out an indenture I'd no wish for. Nay, the first chance I get I'll be on my way."

"Suppose you're caught?" Wasn't a flogging enough to stop him?

"That's a chance I must take." His jaw was set.

"Where will you go?" Surely he must have some plan.

"To Boston or another seaport where I can take ship for Scotland." His voice caressed the word.

"Is someone there waiting for you?" It was all she could do to keep the jealousy out of her tone.

He gave her a quick look. "Neither kith nor kin. But 'tis my ain land. I like it there."

She could think of a dozen pitfalls. Weren't ships carefully inspected for runaways before sailing? Ross might not realize it, but his Scottish burr was still so strong he'd be suspect the minute he opened his mouth. Wasn't there often a reward offered for escaped servants? Surely someone would turn him in for a few pounds.

She started to warn him, but the stony look on his face deterred her. No matter what she said, he'd not listen. He'd set his mind on getting free, and until he himself changed there was naught she could do.

Debby returned, walking with careful steps, carrying a bowl brimful of milk. When she had vanished into the barn, he said, "Anoka plans on going to Boston soon. He has an errand there that's unco important to him. I'll go with him if I can."

He could say no more, for Debby returned, joyfully announcing that the dog was drinking the milk and had wagged her tail in thanks. Ross hurried off to drive the team back to the pits for more charcoal. Joanna followed Debby to the house, her spirits low. Hammersmith would not be the same without Ross. If only he would listen to her!

The next two weeks saw as much activity within the Iron Master's house as without. While wheels turned, bellows blew, and furnaces roared at the Iron Works, brooms swept, dusters flew, and brushes scrubbed at every corner of the house. Joanna was given the task of helping Dame Forrest with her bedchamber. Particular to the point of fussiness, the older woman supervised every move. First the bed had to be stripped, the feather mattresses plumped and spread in the sun, and the covers washed. The bed hangings must be brushed with care lest their appliquéd motifs be harmed. The ropes crisscrossing the bedstead must be tightened with a bed jack to take out the sag.

Then Joanna must polish every piece of furniture, even the spinning wheel and loom. As she rubbed the various parts of the loom, Dame Forrest named them—the rollers to which the threads of the warp were attached, the harness and heddles that lifted and separated the threads of the warp, the shuttle that carried the thread of the weft across, and the laid, with reeds set into it like the teeth of a comb, that pressed the newly woven thread against the cloth. There was also a stretcher that spread the fabric out and kept the ends from chafing. Carvings of birds and flowers decorated the stretcher.

"I brought the loom with me from England," said Dame Forrest. "My husband had it made for me, and I could not bear to think of alien hands working on it. I was not so lame then, and thought a change of climate might improve my condition. Alas, it's worsened the stiffness, and now I can't so much as throw the shuttle. Margaret tells me I should give the loom away; it takes up space here that could be used for other things. But I keep hoping that one day I may weave again." She surveyed her knotted hands ruefully.

Joanna studied the red and white squares of the fabric. A sudden thought struck her. "If I sat at the loom, could you tell me what to do to finish this cloth?"

For long minutes Dame Forrest was silent. Then she said slowly, "It might be possible. Help me to my chair, child."

When she was installed beside the loom, and Joanna was seated on its bench, she directed, "Place your feet on the pedals, so. Now open the shed by pressing the right pedal. That's it. See the tunnel between the threads of the warp? Now place the shuttle between the two layers of threads and throw it through. Gently, but with enough force to carry it most of the way across. Oh, you must help it along. Just put your fingers through the warp and shove it a little. There."

Joanna extracted the shuttle triumphantly and pulled the thread taut.

"That's too tight," warned the dame. "Ease up on it a bit, or you'll have an uneven fabric."

Then Joanna pulled the laid toward her and saw its teeth magically push the new thread against the cloth.

"Now, start all over again," ordered the dame. "Remember, you push down on the left pedal this time. That lifts alternate threads of the warp."

There was a fascination to the different sets of motions that kept Joanna at the loom a long time. "Look," she cried at last, "I've finished a set of squares. Now do I change the thread in the shuttle?"

"That's right," said Dame Forrest approvingly. "Just take a spindle off the filling rack there on the left side of the frame."

So absorbed were they both in the weaving that they did not hear the sound of the iron knocker on the front door. Debby came running up the stairs.

"Joanna, Mamma wants you to answer the door, please."

Reluctantly Joanna got up from the loom and descended the staircase, still absorbed in the intricacies of heddle and shuttle and laid. The iron knocker banged in a rapid rat-tat, as if at an impatient touch. Just inside the door Ruff poised stiffly, fur bristling, a growl rumbling deep in his throat.

"Down, Ruff," she said, putting one hand on his collar. As she started to open the door, Ruff raised his head, slipped out of her grasp, and planted himself in the open doorway, barking fiercely.

The man outside backed away. His close-set eyes were narrowed to slits; his mouth curled in a snarl. He put one hand on a pistol stuck in his belt.

"I'm here to see the Iron Master, if that beast will let me," he announced angrily.

Where had Joanna seen this man before? Where had she heard his voice? Some faint memory sent prickles of fear up her spine. He meant no good here. His evil intent was as clear as the rank odor of his garments. Ruff felt it too. He continued his warning bark.

"You can find Mr. Gifford at the works," she said shortly and began to close the door.

"I've already been to the works. They told me he'd come here. If this wasn't the only iron works around, I'd take my trade elsewhere. What ails Gifford? Be Abner Leach's money not good enough for him?"

Abner Leach. Joanna's memory returned, clear-cut and terrifying. This was the captain of the *Hydra,* the ship from which the Indian woman had leaped to her death in Boston Harbor. She drew back in dismay.

Behind her she heard rapid footsteps and the Iron Master's voice raised inquiringly. "Is someone looking for me?"

He'd hardly reached the doorway when Captain Leach burst out, "Do you want my trade, or not? The girl here told me you weren't at home."

"I've just come in by the other door," said Mr. Gifford curtly. He put an authoritative hand on Ruff's collar, turned to Joanna. "Best shut this dog in the keeping room," he said. "I'll take care of the man."

It took all Joanna's strength to haul Ruff away from the door. He planted his legs firmly, his fur still bristling, his growl erupting in short barks. While she struggled, she heard Mr. Gifford ask, "What business have you with the Iron Works?"

"I've an order for you," announced Abner Leach. "A dozen sets of manacles and an equal number of leg irons, all of the heaviest weight. When can they be ready?"

"Not before a month. I've orders piled up ahead waiting to be filled."

By then she had reached the keeping room and pulled Ruff inside. She shut the door and leaned against it, shaking. There was nothing extraordinary about manacles and leg irons. Many ships had them for restraining prisoners. Why, then, had she so deep a foreboding of evil? She could feel it closing about her heart like an icy hand. Should she tell Mr. Gifford what she knew of this man? Warn him to have no dealings with Leach? Almost as soon as the idea came to her mind she rejected it. She imagined she could hear Mr. Gifford's reply, cool and logical. It's no crime to buy an Indian slave. If it were, some of the colony's leaders would be found guilty. As for the woman's drowning herself, she might have slipped and fallen by accident. Mr. Gifford would not refuse to deal with Captain Leach. He was here to sell iron, not to question a man's character.

No, there'd be no point in telling him. How could she explain that she knew beyond any doubt that the Indian woman had ended her life from grief at losing her child? And that Abner Leach was the essence of all evil? She'd felt it strongly that day on the wharf, and even more so these few minutes ago. Animals had an instinctive perception of evil, she'd heard. She was sure of it now. She knelt down and put her arms around Ruff. He whined unhappily, his head against her throat, as if responding to her thoughts.

14

The Passenger Pigeons

Days of rain ushered in the month of May. Lonely and fretful, Debby tagged at Joanna's heels for hours, the wooden doll in her arms. One afternoon when the keeping room had been tidied after the noonday meal, and Huldah was snoring by the fire, Joanna looked at Debby's wistful face and whispered, "It's time we made your poppet a gown. Can you find some scraps of cloth?"

The child's face brightened. "I'll see," she said, and ran out of the room. In a few minutes she was back with a sack of pieces, bits of satin and paduasoy, lace and braid. "Grandmother said I could choose what I like," she explained.

Joanna fingered the rich materials, excitement mounting within her. She would make a gown fit for a princess! She took down the scissors and began cutting, while Debby watched at her elbow.

The following afternoon she slipped the completed gown over the doll's stiff body and held it out. Debby squealed with delight. Huldah stirred from her nap and gave a grudging word of praise. Joanna could not stifle a thrill of satisfaction. The gown was of royal-blue satin with a pointed bodice. The underskirt was of crimson taffeta, quilted, and the sleeves were slashed to reveal glimpses of crimson. A broad lace falling band tied with narrow crimson ribbons finished the neck. If there had been more ribbon, she would have put bows on the sleeves as well.

Debby pranced from the room, holding the doll at arm's length. For a moment Joanna panicked. Mistress Gifford would be displeased that she had spent her time thus when she might have been polishing pewter. Guiltily she took up a piece of soft leather and began to rub at a platter.

A few minutes later the door opened. Joanna braced herself for a scolding. The mistress had the doll in her hand.

"Why did you not tell me you had such skill with the needle?" she asked. For once her voice was not heavy with condemnation. "Here I have been scouring the countryside for a seamstress when I already had one under my own roof."

Joanna stood silent. What was there to say—that Mistress Gifford had never taken the time to learn anything about her?

"There's a deal of sewing to be done," the mistress went on. "I'd like well for you to begin on it tomorrow."

"And who's to help me with the work?" inquired Huldah. "I'm not minded to do double duty while she sits and plies a needle." By the tone of her voice, mending and sewing were games of leisure.

"I'll get one of John Butt's girls in to help," declared the mistress with finality.

And so it was settled. Apple-cheeked Eliza Butt at fourteen was strong and willing and happy to escape from the care of seven younger Butts. Though Joanna still helped with the cooking and bedmaking, she was relieved of the drudgery of drawing water, scouring iron pots, tending fires, scrubbing floors, and churning butter. As soon as the light was strong enough, she settled herself by the window and took up needle and thimble.

Mostly there were split seams and tears to repair. One day Joanna was working on a violet silk when the mistress came into the room.

"Don't spend much time on that," she cautioned. " 'Tis hopelessly out of fashion. My latest letter from London said that no one wears stiff whisks now. And the sleeves are all wrong."

Joanna inspected the dress critically. "If I changed the neckline, put on a falling band of lace, and made virago sleeves for it, 'twould be modish enough."

"Could you make the sleeves?" the mistress asked eagerly.

"I can try," Joanna said. She climbed to the garret and took her saffron gown from the chest where she had placed it months ago. At once strange and familiar, the dress loosed a flood of memories. She fingered the sleeves while her tears welled. This was no time for self-pity or for looking backward, she told herself. She had come up here to study the sleeve so she could copy it. Resolutely she gauged the amount of goods needed, the placement of gathers, and put the gown away. It was part of her past. It had no place in the present save as a help to her work.

But she could not resist stroking the lustrous material with fond fingers before closing the heavy lid.

By week's end the violet gown had been refurbished. The mistress was delighted. She even praised Joanna and said she would wear the gown to meeting.

The Sabbath dawned with sparkling clarity and sudden warmth. When John Butt brought in the milk, he left the door open, announcing, " 'Tis warmer without than within."

When the time drew near to leave for meeting, Debby was running in and out, a bright little figure in her scarlet dress. Mistress Gifford descended the stairs, her gown of violet silk turned back to display a rose-colored quilted petticoat. Joanna regarded her critically. She did look modish, she had to admit. The virago sleeves had worked wonders.

Mistress Gifford was saying with ill-concealed pleasure, "I believe it's too warm to wear a cloak today."

" 'Twould be a pity to cover your gown," said her husband admiringly.

Joanna could hardly believe her ears. What had happened to the Giffords' customary bickering? She was so amazed at their amiability she could almost forget her own longing for a new dress. The brown wool was hot and itchy. How she would like something thin and cool—and pretty.

The meetinghouse looked as gay as a flower garden this first Sabbath that was warm enough for the ladies to go without cloaks. Joanna could see curious glances flying from one woman to another. Mistress Gifford, she decided with no small degree of satisfaction, was easily the most modish person present. Nearly everyone else looked like the season before last.

When Mr. Whiting had mounted the pulpit and was waiting for silence, the rustling and crackling of satins and taffetas was clearly audible. Turning toward the ladies, he said with caustic emphasis, " 'And why take ye thought for raiment? Consider the lilies of the field, how they grow; they toil not, neither do they spin: And yet I say unto you, That even Solomon in all his glory was not arrayed like one of these.' "

For an hour he attacked the folly of fashion, the sinfulness of pride in fine dress, the wickedness of lace and such fripperies. He said that the love of luxury was nugiperous.

Huldah turned a puzzled frown on Joanna. "Nugiperous? What tribe is that? Algonquin?"

Joanna could only shake her head, though she suspected the word had more to do with vanity than Indians. Did she fancy that the women in the front rows no longer held their heads quite so high? Was it her imagination, or were some of them shrinking down on their benches?

The meeting over, Joanna half expected the women to scurry homeward, ashamed of their fine clothing. But groups clustered about the doorway as usual. Wapaket strode among them, the skirts of his yellow coat flapping against his deerskin leggings.

Joanna looked for Ross. Sometimes he stopped to ask after the puppies or the state of the woodpile. Today he merely waved a hand in greeting, then hurried off with the other Scots. They had a good distance to go to eat their dinner and come back for the next service.

Joanna watched Yaweta leave the Whitings and talk for

a few minutes with Anoka. Then the Indian girl walked hesitantly over to Joanna.

"Mistress Whiting says I may walk with you. Do you wish me to?" Her dark eyes were questioning, her smile timorous.

"There's naught I'd like better," said Joanna quickly. Huldah drew back, grasping Debby's hand, but the child pulled away and clung to Joanna. Bristling with indignation, Huldah moved away toward Goodwife Talbot.

"Have you been to visit your mother lately?" asked Joanna, slowing her steps. If they lagged behind, they would not have to listen to Huldah and the Talbots complaining about Indians.

"Not for a fortnight," replied Yaweta, "but Anoka tells me she is well. I cannot help thinking about her, and my thoughts are not happy."

"It's too bad your father cast her off," said Joanna.

Instantly Yaweta rose to his defense. "He did but what he thought was right for a Christian," she said, her tawny cheeks burning.

"That's so," agreed Joanna mildly. When would she learn to hold her tongue?

"I am troubled about my father too," said Yaweta. "In the Bible it says to take no thought for your body, what ye shall drink and what ye shall eat. But have you seen how very thin he has become? I fear he may grow ill."

"Surely he'll eat when he's hungry," said Joanna.

"I do not know if he has anything in his house to eat," said Yaweta. "The Bible also says to give away that which thou hast, and he has given away everything except the clothes he wears. He has almost nothing left. I know we should do as the Bible says, but my father obeys in more ways than white men. I do not see them going without food or drink, or giving away all that they own. It is very hard for me to understand."

So engrossed were the girls in their conversation that they had dropped some distance behind the other villagers. Debby, finding their conversation dull, ran to catch up with her mother. The girls heard hoarse shouts and guttural cries from the road behind them. Turning, they saw Wapaket attempting to break away from a group of Indian men. There were three, younger and apparently stronger than he.

One uttered a few contemptuous words and hit Wapaket a heavy blow on the side of the head. For a moment he staggered, as if trying to remain upright, then fell to the ground. Yaweta ran toward him, Joanna following her. He had covered his head with his arms and was lying nearly motionless.

As the girls drew near they could hear a young brave say, "Wapaket is like squaw. No fight like Indian."

Muffled words came from Wapaket. "Me good Christian. Is wrong to fight."

"Wapaket not good Indian. Wapaket not good white man." The brave gave the supine figure a sharp kick. A second Indian also kicked the older man. The third spat on him. Then they walked away.

Yaweta helped her father to his feet and brushed off his yellow coat. "Let me bring you to the Whitings," she begged. "They will give you dinner."

He pushed her aside. "No need food," he said, "need prayer." He knelt down by the roadside, mumbling to himself.

"Come, Father, or you will be hungry." Yaweta tugged at his arm.

He shook her off. "Go to minister. Learn Christian way. Go."

The girls had no choice but to leave him there, deep in prayer. Each one troubled by her thoughts, they hurried to their homes.

In the afternoon Joanna and the Giffords were halfway to the meetinghouse when the sky began to darken and there came a sound as of wind rushing through the trees. Joanna looked up, expecting to see storm clouds. Instead she saw a dark mass approaching. It filled the sky, a throbbing, beating mass of birds. She clutched at Huldah's arm, pointing upward.

The Iron Master had halted in his tracks. "The passenger pigeons are early this year," he said. " 'Tis well our fields are not yet seeded, else we'd have it all to do over."

"Think you we should return home?" inquired his wife nervously.

"No," he said, "the flock will pass over while we're in meeting."

The birds were overhead now. They formed a rushing canopy of blue and white and wine shades. Joanna stared, fascinated, but Debby burst into tears. "I'm afraid," she sobbed.

"A great girl like you," scoffed Huldah.

"You must control yourself, Deborah," admonished her mother.

Joanna put a comforting arm about the shaking shoulders. What if the birds should check their flight and descend? It was a frightening prospect. She could well understand how the child felt. Mr. Gifford, too, must have shared her anxiety.

"Just a few rods more," he said. "We'll soon be under cover."

During the whole afternoon service the throb of beating wings sounded overhead, though there was a full two-hour sermon preached by Mr. Thomas Cobbet, Mr. Whiting's assistant.

"'Honor thy father and thy mother,'" he said, "be he or she poor or rich, noble or ignoble, high or low, of meaner parts or of more accomplished abilities, comely and personable or deformed and in stature more despicable, yea, be they of better and sweeter tempers or be they of a more harsh, hasty, and rigid disposition, yet as servants must be subject to their masters with all fear, not only to the good and gentle but also the froward, so must children much rather give honor to their parents, whether of better or worser tempers.

"Honor is fourfold," he declared. "It involves respect, reverence, obedience, and recompense. Parents were unwearied in their labors for their children's good. It would be a monstrous thing if children should not now do all that ever they can to maintain their decaying, decrepit, exhausted parents."

Joanna could see Wapaket sitting as usual near the front of the meetinghouse, the Puritans on either side edging as far away from him as possible. She could imagine the turmoil in Yaweta's mind as she listened to the sermon. How could she respect and revere this bizarre savage? Or obey and recompense him? Yet there was something awe-inspiring about his fanatical observance of Christian precepts.

Once the service was over and she had quit the meeting-house, Joanna forgot everything except the sight before her eyes. The gigantic flock of pigeons had recently alighted on the ground. A nearby meadow was alive with a moving coverlet of blue metallic feathers glinting in the sunlight. Some pigeons roosted on the meetinghouse roof. Others clustered on branches of trees.

Men hurried their families home with all possible speed. There would be pigeon pie tonight, and roasted, stewed, baked, and fried pigeon for days to come.

Joanna could not take her eyes from the birds. How graceful they were, with their long, graduated tail feathers! And how colorful, with their slate-blue backs and wine-colored breasts, brightened by iridescent rings around their necks! As in the morning, she and Yaweta lagged behind the others. They were the last of the congregation walking along the road, save for Wapaket, who stalked along behind them.

Just ahead was a frame house, the maple tree in its front yard a fluttering mass of pigeons. So thick were the birds that the branches seemed covered with blue feathers.

A man came from the barn, carrying a long pole. With heavy blows he swept the birds from their perches, clubbing them as they fell to the ground. Two boys appeared and began to cram the dead birds into sacks.

Revulsion swept over Joanna. Yet she continued to watch, rooted by an ugly fascination. Now Wapaket came abreast of the house. He raised his head. His features took on an expression of righteous indignation.

"White man much wicked to kill on Sabbath," he shouted, his guttural voice lending a strange accent to each word.

"Be off with ye!" grunted the farmer, taking another swipe at the birds. He turned toward Wapaket, the pole in his hands. "If ye mind not your own affairs, I'll give ye a poke with this." He brandished the pole near Wapaket's face.

The Indian stood his ground. "God will punish white man for sins," he said solemnly. Yaweta took his hand and attempted to draw him away.

The farmer had knocked most of the birds off the lower branches. Now he urged his sons to climb the tree to catch the pigeons roosting higher up. One shinnied up and started out along a limb. Suddenly there was a sharp crack, a form accompanied by feathers hurtled through the air, and the boy landed on the ground. He lay there, moaning. The man bent over him, then rose and shook a fist at Wapaket.

"He would have been all right had you not come along," he said venomously.

Wapaket regarded him stoically. "Now white man know it wrong to kill on Lord's day," he said pontifically and moved on.

Frightened, Joanna hurried along beside Yaweta. It seemed almost as if Wapaket had the power of an evil spirit, bringing about the boy's accident. Even though they could see the boy rise and walk into the house, both girls were deeply troubled.

All the way back to the minister's house, Yaweta walked as one in a trance, staring at the skyline, wringing her hands.

"I do not know what to do," she said. "I wish that I might help him, but I do not know how."

"What does Mr. Whiting say?" asked Joanna.

"He says it is too bad the world is not yet ready to accept Christianity as fully as my father does. But that does not help my father now. This morning I feared that he would die from his own neglect. Now I fear that he will die at the hands of his enemies. He has many—both red men and white."

15

Anoka's Hoard

Springtime wrought magical changes in and about the village of Hammersmith. True, the vast chimney of the smelting furnace poured forth smoke and sparks in an unending torrent, and the hammer lent its staccato din to daylight hours. But green grass covered the hillside, lacy leaves feathered the branches, and flowers lent splashes of color to meadow and woodland.

Never had Joanna heard so many birds. Before the watchman's horn sounded the birds began their signaling of the day. The first tentative peep would be joined by others until the air was filled with joyous song.

The puppies grew into warm, cuddly, wiggling balls of fur. They learned to climb out of the straw-filled box and staggered about the barn on wobbly legs. With needle-sharp teeth they nipped at Joanna's fingers, bit Debby's shoe latchets. Soon, John Butt said, they'd be big enough to leave their mother.

One morning, after delivering a load of charcoal, Ross

came to the Iron Master's house with a message. The Widow Talbot was ready to make her year's supply of soap and would take it kindly if Joanna could be spared to help. Mistress Gifford acceded readily.

Joanna rode on the wagon seat beside Ross, a clean piece of canvas protecting her dress from the black charcoal dust. In her lap she held a puppy that John Butt had sent out for the Talbot boys.

"Mind you watch him with that cat around," he cautioned. "If it takes a dislike to the pup, it might scratch his eyes out."

For a while the pup wriggled restlessly, then settled down on her lap, his round head resting on tiny paws. Joanna lifted him in her hands and sniffed the warm, sweet fragrance of his downy fur.

Soon they came to the wood road that led to the charcoal pits. "It lacks an hour yet of noontime," said Ross. "Would ye care to see the pits?"

She hesitated. "They're likely just dirty, ashy holes in the ground."

"Nay, lass, they're great high things, like giant beehives. I was unco surprised at the first one I saw. Let me show you."

He clucked to the horse, and they entered the wood. The smell of smoke came faintly to their nostrils. Soon they reached the clearing where the Scots had cut wood during the winter. Cord after cord was neatly stacked. Here the colliers got their supply of wood. The smell of smoke grew stronger. A short distance farther on they came within sight of a circular mound covered with turf and dirt. From a small aperture in the top rose a thin spiral of blue smoke.

"Where is the charcoal?" asked Joanna, mystified.

"Inside the mound," replied Ross. "It's built up in layers, stick by stick, billet by billet. Look over there; the men have begun another."

Nearby a half-dozen men were constructing a second mound, laying pieces of wood in concentric layers like the spokes of a wheel. Each layer was smaller than the one beneath. The whole resembled a giant mosaic, the colors of the wood blending in a pattern of tan and brown.

It was good to see the Scots again. She waved and spoke to each by name; then Ross turned the wagon and they lumbered off. They had reached the clearing where the wood was stacked when an Indian glided out from behind a tree and stood in their path. He wore deerskin leggings and shirt, with an eagle feather in his long hair. For a moment Joanna gasped in fear, but when Ross pulled up the horses and spoke she recognized Anoka. He carried a leather sack, long and narrow, and Joanna knew it was heavy from the way its weight pulled the strings taut.

The young Indian stepped to the rear of the wagon. He beckoned to Ross. "Come," he said and upended the sack and poured out a stream of shillings and pence upon the rough boards. A few dropped through a crack. He gravely stooped to retrieve them.

"How much here?" he asked Ross. "You tell me."

Joanna jumped down from the wagon seat, set the puppy on the ground, and joined the two young men. She couldn't remember seeing so many coins all at once ever before.

"Where did you get all this?" inquired Ross.

"Chop wood, get two shillings for one cord. Pile wood in cords, get six shillings for one score."

"You must have worked two or three years for this," said Ross. "Didn't you spend any of your money?"

"Not spend. Keep," said Anoka. "You count now."

"Bein' a Scot, I thought I knew about thrift," Ross said, laughing, "but ye go the Scots one better, Anoka. I'll count it gladly for ye. Twelve pennies make a shilling, and twenty shillings make a pound. We'll divide the shillings and pence; that'll make it easier."

Joanna joined him, placing the coins in neat piles. There was more than five pounds, she saw. If only this money were hers, she could take it to Mr. Gifford and pay off her indenture. Was Ross having a similar thought?

His black eyes intent, Anoka was watching Ross count.

"Ye've seven pounds, three shillings, and sixpence," announced Ross admiringly.

"Is enough?" inquired Anoka.

"Enough for what?" Joanna burst out. She couldn't contain her curiosity another minute.

Anoka regarded her somberly. "To buy Indian woman slave," he replied.

"Oh, Anoka, how can you think of such a thing?" she asked. "Is it not bad enough that white men take Indians as slaves?" She was about to add "and that Indians make slaves of white captives," but bit off the words.

"Tell her, Anoka," urged Ross. "Tell her who it is you want to buy."

"Anoka's mother is slave. Me buy from white man," said the Indian painfully.

Joanna let her breath out in a long sigh. "Where is she?"

"He thinks she's in Boston," said Ross. "He heard she was captured by a man named Grubb—Jeremiah Grubb."

A faint memory flickered in Joanna's mind like a spark in a dying fire. It glowed for an instant, then faded.

"Is enough?" Anoka repeated anxiously.

"I dinna ken for sure. Some bring ten or twenty pounds, some less. It depends." He stopped. It depends on whether she's well and strong, thought Joanna. If she's old and weak, her price will be lower.

Anoka scooped up the coins, returned them to the bag. "Get more, then go," he announced and glided off into the woods as silently as he had appeared.

Ross's face bore traces of disappointment. He's upset because his running off to Boston with Anoka is delayed, thought Joanna. She was far from disappointed. Ross would be in Hammersmith a little longer, at least. She picked up the puppy and climbed onto the wagon seat.

As they drew near the Scots' house, Ross pulled on the reins, and the wagon came to a stop. In the grass beside the lane Phineas lay flat on his stomach, watching a colony of ants. The puppy in Joanna's arms gave a squeak. Instantly Phineas was on his feet.

"A dog?" he breathed, his eyes like stars. He put his hand out and touched the small head reverently. "Can I hold him?"

He picked up the furry mite, held it against his cheek. The puppy nuzzled against him, then squirmed impatiently. Phineas set him gently on the ground, where he ran about uncertainly. Each wobbly step, each movement of the tiny pointed tail, each wrinkling of the small nose Phineas regarded with rapture. A squirrel ran down a nearby tree trunk, arched its tail, and threatened, "Cuk-cuk-cuk!"

Terrified, the pup sought refuge between Phineas's feet. The boy picked him up, his face shining with sheer unadulterated joy.

"Want me to watch him for you?" he asked Ross.

"He's for you and Hiram," said Ross. "John Butt sent him to you."

"For us, our very own?" If Phineas had been happy before, he now appeared to have achieved heavenly bliss. His wide-set hazel eyes shone; his mouth curved in a smile of infinite happiness. "I'll take good care of him," he announced gravely.

At the door Maura greeted Joanna with a cry of welcome. "'Tis that glad I am to see you," she exclaimed. "I get downright lonely for some female talk. All these men are fine, but now and then I hanker to have another woman about."

"A good time for me to bid ye farewell," said Ross with a twinkle. "I ken when I'm unwelcome." With a wave of his hand, he drove back toward the woods.

Maura drew Joanna into the house, talking all the way. Tomorrow they'd make the soap, she said. She had already leached a barrel of wood ashes, pouring water on the top, a little at a time, to drip slowly through. The men had set up two stakes and a crosspiece out by the barn so she could make the soap outdoors. It was too messy a job to do indoors. Besides, the fat, some of it rancid, had a strong odor best kept outdoors.

In the evening Ross brought out his bagpipes and gave Joanna another lesson. As before, she had difficulty producing even a squeak at first, but with practice learned how to sound a few notes properly.

Rain the next day changed Maura's plans. The men went off as usual. A little wet didn't interfere with coaling or bringing up supplies of wood to the colliers. Maura wasn't so hard up for soap that she had to stand around in the rain coaxing a fire. There was plenty to do inside.

Phineas hovered over the puppy, watching his every movement and keeping a careful eye on the cat. He had slept in the keeping room, curled up on a pallet beside the pup's basket. Joanna was sure the pup had spent more time tucked inside Phineas's shirt than he had in the basket. The cat, strangely, showed more curiosity than antagonism. Each time it approached the pup, Phineas placed a restraining, kindly hand on each. The cat sniffed at the little dog, purred, and licked his soft fur with a rasping tongue. Phineas's voice matched the purr. "Ye'll be good friends," he said contentedly.

"I've something to show you," said Maura proudly to Joanna. She disappeared into her chamber and returned a minute later, her apron caught up at the corners, filled with hanks of yarn. She turned a medley of soft colors out on the table. Some of the yarn was deep green, some soft brown. A large part was a deep blue, and a few skeins were bright yellow.

"The colors are beautiful," exclaimed Joanna admiringly. "Did you dye them yourself?"

"That I did," said Maura. "Most of the dyes I made, too. The yellow's from onion skins, the brown and green from bark and moss. Indigo made the blue—I got that from the peddler. There's something else, too, a length of cloth I have just back from the weaver. I'd thought of making a dress for myself, this one's so worn. But I'm that clumsy with sewing, I'm loath to put scissors to the goods."

She brought a length of soft green wool and held it up against herself. "Think you 'tis a good color?"

" 'Tis vastly becoming," Joanna said sincerely. The green set off the golden glints of Maura's hair far better than the salt-and-pepper of her present gown. "I'll help you make it, if you like."

"Would you, now?" Maura's smile flashed. "I was hopin' you'd offer, you're that handy with the needle."

All day, while the rain dripped outside, Joanna cut and basted and fitted. While Joanna stitched, Maura busied herself about the house, singing snatches of melody. Joanna was fitting a sleeve in place when Maura murmured, "I wonder, now, if Duncan likes green."

"Duncan?" asked Joanna, puzzled.

Maura colored. "I was just wondering," she said. "John liked mulberry, but 'twas never my color." She hummed a tune.

So Maura was thinking of Duncan. But hadn't she said she'd not marry again?

"I thought you said you'd have no man telling you what food you could put in your sons' mouths," Joanna said.

"And so I did"—Maura laughed—"before I knew Duncan Muir. But he's a man would see that they were fed, and fed well, though everyone else went hungry. He's that fond of the boys I wonder sometimes if he's not more interested in them than in meself."

"Has he asked you to marry him?" asked Joanna eagerly.

" 'Tis no secret." Maura nodded, smiling. "Of course

we've to wait till he's worked out his time, but that will
pass." Her happiness was contagious.

Joanna couldn't feel surprised. From the very first she
had known that Duncan and Maura were a match for each
other. With him Maura threw off the reserve she'd learned
at the Talbots'. With Duncan she could dance, kicking
the flounce of her scarlet petticoat about.

"There's good land to be had in the north," said Maura.
"Duncan wants to go there and build a place for us."

"Aren't you afraid of Indians?" asked Joanna.

"Not with Duncan," declared Maura with serene confidence.

When the men came back that night, Joanna noted the
special look Duncan gave Maura, the interest with which
he studied Hiram's carving of a frow handle, and the
tenderness with which he observed Phineas and the pup.
She could imagine him felling trees in the wilderness,
building a home for Maura and the boys. If she were
Maura, she'd be wild with impatience. But Maura had
learned the secret of finding contentment in each day.

When the evening meal was cleared away, Ross again
instructed Joanna in playing the bagpipes. By dint of
great effort she succeeded in forcing out a series of sounds
that Ross termed passable.

For hours he kept her working at it, until her lungs were
weary with blowing and her arm and shoulder tired from
forcing the air out of the bag.

By bedtime she had mastered a series of notes and felt
a rush of pride when Ross exclaimed, "All ye need is practice, lass. Ye'll be a piper yet!"

The next morning was fair, the air washed sparkling
clear. Duncan built a fire under the framework. Maura

measured the grease, adding a quantity of lye. Ross and Duncan placed the crossbar under the handle of the pot and raised it until it rested on the supports. Maura took up a long wooden bar with a shorter one set at right angles to it, and began stirring the contents of the pot.

"We'll be back at noon to lend you a hand," said Duncan.

Maura and Joanna took turns stirring the soap. When Maura judged it of the right consistency, they let the fire die down.

After the men had lifted the pot off the fire, Joanna and Maura ladled the thick brown liquid into boxes lined with old pieces of cloth. It cooled quickly into thick cream-colored slabs. Maura would cut it into cakes in a few days, when it was solid enough to handle. Then she would stack the bars in a dry place where the air could circulate around them until the soap had seasoned enough for use.

There was time before supper for Joanna to finish Maura's dress. While she worked, she told Maura about Dame Forrest's loom and her efforts to finish the dame's coverlet.

"Now I know how I can repay you for helping me with the dress," cried Maura. "I'll spin and dye ye some wool, and ye can weave a length of cloth for a new gown for yerself. What color would ye like?"

How she would love a new gown! One of greenish blue, her favorite color. This shapeless brown thing she'd been wearing all winter was at best a covering. She was fingering the wools when a thought struck her.

Here were dark blue, green, yellow—the colors of the McCrae tartan, except for the line of red that crisscrossed here and there. Ross's plaid was threadbare. Could she weave a copy of the tartan from wools like these? All that was lacking was red, but Maura had offered her red dye months ago. In a trice she made up her mind. She could wait for a new dress. Ross had more need of a plaid.

"If you've still got that red dye," she said, "I've a use for it." And she told Maura her plan.

When the evening meal was finished, Maura shooed Joanna and Ross out the door. "I'll tend to the washing-up," she said. "You get along whilst 'tis yet light."

They took the short cut beside the pond above the Iron Works. The surface of the water was smooth, the air cool and soft. Above the dull roar of the giant furnace, birds sang their evening chorus. Wild lilies of the valley grew thickly under the trees, their white flowers forming a tufted pattern against the shiny green of their leaves. Birch trees were fringed with golden fronds. On the ground beneath, pink lady's-slippers bloomed in fragile beauty. Blueberry bushes bore creamy cups of blossom.

A short distance ahead of them, a slender figure in a green gown with a crimson fichu stepped out of the woods onto the path. There was no mistaking the head held high, the graceful walk.

"Yaweta," called Joanna.

The girl turned, pleasure lighting her face. A ruddy tinge colored her high cheekbones. She looked inquiringly at Joanna's companion.

"This is Ross McCrae," Joanna said.

"I know," said Yaweta shyly. "He is a friend to Anoka. I have seen him at the meetinghouse."

The three walked along together.

"I have been visiting my mother," explained Yaweta. "I stayed longer than usual, and I must hurry back to the Whitings'."

"Is your mother well?"

"She is almost ill from loneliness," explained Yaweta sadly. "I did not like to leave her, but my father says I must remain at the minister's and be a good Christian. So I will do as he says."

Soon they had passed the dam and followed the canal to the crest of the hill near the loading platform. Coming toward them was a small wiry man with a rolling gait and sharp-featured face. With instant distaste, Joanna recognized him. It was Abner Leach. Again she felt a prickle of fear. Yaweta, who had been walking beside her, fell back a step or two.

"Can you show me where to find the Iron Master?" asked Leach. "I've been to the house, and they told me he was at the forge, wherever that might be. I've come to pick up some things I ordered a month ago." His small eyes darted to Joanna and Yaweta, then fastened on Ross.

"I'll show you," said the Scot. "This way." He led the man down the stone steps set in the hillside.

As they descended, Abner Leach raised his voice above the din of the furnace. "A good, healthy-seeming squaw, that. Be there more of them about?"

Joanna flinched at his words. Did he think Yaweta was a slave? She hoped he'd take his manacles and leg irons and never come back again. She put her arm through Yaweta's and hurried her along. The farther away they got from Abner Leach, the better she'd feel.

16

Muster Day

Wild strawberries ripened in June. One day Joanna and
Debby went berrying in company with the Whiting girls
and Yaweta. All afternoon they gathered the fragile red
globes, some as large as their thumbs, on the bank of the
Saugus River. At day's end, sunburned and sticky, their
lips and fingers stained red, they returned home, bearing
large baskets filled with fragrant berries.

"You've picked a wondrous lot," said Huldah in a burst
of unwonted praise. "There'll be enough for preserves, and
tarts for Muster Day."

Muster Day. Joanna had heard of little else all afternoon. It would take place the day after tomorrow on the
common ground in front of the meetinghouse. Every able-
bodied man must be present to march and drill and shoot
at targets. Boys from ten to sixteen would be exercised
in the use of small guns, half-pikes, and bows and arrows.
Wives and children would go along to admire and ap-

plaud. What was the point of men's marching and drilling with no one to watch and cheer?

At noonday there would be a picnic—and such a picnic! Each housewife brought her specialties. Dishes were shared with friends and neighbors. It was a veritable feast. Joanna would love it all.

Muster Day dawned in a miracle of sunshine and birdsong. As soon as breakfast had been cleared away, Huldah and Joanna set about filling baskets. There were bread and cold meat to slice, a roast chicken to cut up, and early lettuce to be gathered from the garden.

Soon they were on their way, part of an informal, straggling parade of families. It was like the Sabbath, but with an air of festivity and anticipation.

"May I have just a little corner of a strawberry tart?" begged Debby when they had gone about halfway.

"Not now, Deborah," said her mother. "You must learn to control your appetite."

The strawberry tarts! Huldah threw Joanna a stricken glance. She'd put them high on the dresser shelf, out of Debby's reach. "Did you pack them?" she asked Joanna.

"No, but I'll run back for them."

At the house, she looked in on Dame Forrest dozing in her chair. She took down the tarts, packed them in a linen square in a splint basket. One she put on a plate and took in to the dame.

She had picked up the basket and was about to set out again when she heard a fumbling at the back door. Impatiently she swung it wide. Before her stood Ross McCrae, a bundle under one arm and the bagpipes in his hand. At the sight of Joanna, his face flushed with confusion.

"I thought ye'd be gone to the muster."

"Do you usually come a-calling when folks are away?" she asked tartly.

"I was about to leave my bagpipes," he said stiffly. "Ye did say ye'd look after them for me."

Her heart dropped to her boots. So he was really leaving. Of course he'd chosen today, when practically everyone would be at the training ground. No one would miss him till nightfall, and by then he'd be well away from Hammersmith.

"Is Anoka going with you?"

"Nay, but I canna wait for him to save enough silver."

"Are you sure you want to chance it?" she asked.

"I'm not afraid of a flogging." How stiffly he set his jaw!

"But will you be easy in your mind, knowing that any day you might be recognized and returned to the Iron Master?"

"That's for me to decide. All I know is that seven years is too long to spend in a charcoal pit. If I could work in the forge or the slitting mill or at the furnace—but there's nae use even thinkin' about it." He laid the bagpipes down on the table. "I'd best be on my way."

Words choked her. Dared she confess how lonely she'd be without him? Should she tell him how much she'd come to depend upon his quiet understanding? That no one else shared her background of loss and loneliness? But all she could say, in a wooden voice, was, "Do not go, Ross."

He answered briefly, "I must," and turned on his heel. Then he hurried out the door—and straight into the arms of Mr. Whiting!

When the minister had caught his breath, he stood

back and peered closely at Ross. "Bless me," he said, "here's a young man in a hurry. And I do believe the very person I'm looking for."

Ross stared at him, open-mouthed.

"We need some music for the trainbands," said Mr. Whiting. "The fifer is ill of a fever, and the men are discovering that marching without a tune is like a sermon without a prayer. I bethought myself of you and your bagpipes, and came to ask Joanna where you might be found. Do you know some martial airs?"

"Aye," Ross said uncertainly. Joanna could almost see his consternation. While he hesitated, she burst out, "You recall how well he played the lament for Mr. Davison? He can pipe a march every bit as well."

"I had hoped as much." The minister's face lit up.

Ross threw her a steely glance. He was trapped, and he knew it.

"Go fetch your bagpipes," said Mr. Whiting. "The sooner you can get to the training ground, the better."

Joanna darted into the house, picked up the pipes, and handed them to Ross. If Mr. Whiting was surprised, he did not show it.

"Excellent," he said. "We can all walk along together." He led the way toward the common.

Ross gave Joanna a glance of vexation. There goes my chance to run off, it said as clearly as words. A fine help you were, telling how well I can pipe.

She tossed her head. For once she didn't care if Ross was pleased or not. He was still here and would have to remain for the day at least. She could put up with a bit of a glower.

All the way to the parade ground, Mr. Whiting talked.

First he spoke of the goodness of the Lord as evidenced by the song of the birds, the warmth of the sun, and the shade of the trees. Wonderful were the works of the Lord, and marvelous His plans for the children of men, better than ever they dreamed. Ofttimes He seemed to put obstacles in the way, especially in the paths of young folk, but with riper years they would be thankful that His will had prevented them from committing some rash deed.

Joanna could see Ross peering suspiciously at the minister, but Mr. Whiting turned a bland countenance upon him and exclaimed, "What a fine strong body. With those arms you could fell trees."

"That I have, and a good many," declared Ross. His voice held a hint of pride.

"Ah, if I were but young enough to go into the wilderness and make a home there, far from the follies and foibles of mankind."

Joanna found it hard to imagine frail Mr. Whiting with an ax in his hand.

"For the man strong enough to wrest a living from it, there's all the land he can want, enough for him and his sons and his sons' sons," continued Mr. Whiting.

"Aye, 'tis fine for them that be free to take it," said Ross bitterly.

"Many's the man now happy by his fireside, with his fields stretching far on either side, who, like Jacob, had to work for what he wanted."

"Seven years is a long time," said Ross somberly.

"It depends on which end you look at it from. Time's like a spyglass. When you peer through it one way, everything seems larger. And from the other end, all seems smaller. Right now seven years seems endless to you, I've no doubt. But when 'tis over, 'twill seem but a brief span."

"But they'd be seven wasted years," protested Ross.

"Perchance that was what the children of Israel thought when Moses was leading them to the Promised Land. But in their forty years of wandering they grew from a group of slaves to a company of self-governing people. They had lessons to learn, and the Lord kept them in the wilderness until He thought they were ready to live in the land of Canaan."

"But what's a man to learn here that's useful?"

"Felling trees, for one thing. And any skill that will help him to survive in a new country. Hunting and fishing, growing crops, raising cattle. And there's the ironmaking." He turned to Joanna. "There are arts in which a woman should be versed, too."

She could feel her face burning.

"A good housewife is to be prized above rubies. Here in this new land many lives may depend upon her skill in making palatable whatever food there be, in fashioning clothing from wool and flax, in providing home comforts in the midst of peril."

Just ahead was the common, where the men were drilling in a strangely glum fashion. Ross tucked the sheepskin bag under his arm, blew air into it, and turned the valves on the drones as he walked. Weird squawks escaped, then a ripple of minor notes. As they approached the parade ground, he let loose a torrent of martial music that swept through the crowd like an east wind on a sultry day.

The men straightened, shouldering their muskets and marching with new vigor. The young boys threw their half-pikes about in exultation, shouting, "Huzzah!" The captain barked orders with renewed spirit, and the lieutenant stepped briskly about to see that the commands were carried out properly. Even the ladies started humming and beating time to the stirring music of the bagpipes.

Joanna looked about for the Giffords. They were sitting with Mistress Whiting and her girls. Happily she followed the minister across the soft grass, gave the basket of tarts to Huldah, and sank down beside Yaweta. Mistress Whiting leaned over, patted Joanna's hand, and gave her a bright glance. Debby snuggled next to her, her poppet in her arms.

The sun shone with a pleasant warmth. The fragrance of wild roses and evergreens combined with the tang of salt. Song sparrows lifted their voices. Gulls soared and called overhead.

Women moved about from one group to another, chatting and visiting. Children played at hopscotch and blindman's buff. And at noontime the lunch baskets were opened.

There were loaves of crusty bread, wedges of homemade cheese, slices of home-cured ham, and cold meat pasties. There were seed cakes, plum buns, and, best of all, the strawberry tarts, their rich pastry crumbling to release rivulets of crimson sweetness. There were milk and cider for the children and ladies, and stronger potions for the men. As the afternoon wore on, members of the trainbands slaked their thirst with increasing regularity, until the drilling, poorly disciplined at best, resembled a cheerful rout more than a review.

After the morning's excitement, Joanna was content to sit quietly with Yaweta. The Indian girl seemed less troubled than usual. She had visited her mother again yesterday and had found her well. Her father, too, seemed better. She had been praying for God's help, and was confident He would direct her in all her ways.

Maura came by to chat. Phineas had brought his puppy, loath to be parted from it for even a day. He'd named it Tip for the white tip on its tail. The small dog wandered about, nose to ground, now gamboling, now tripping over its own paws.

While the militia filed and presented arms, stood at attention and at ease, Joanna found her eyes ever returning to the piper at their head. For all that he was wearing the rough shirt and breeches of a working man, he carried himself proudly, his shoulders squared and his head thrown back as he poured music from the pipes. The best thing about Muster Day was that Ross was still here, not half a day away with a sentence hanging over him. If only he would decide to remain at Hammersmith. But what would induce him to stay?

While the men gathered for the last formation, the captain approached Ross, who stood not ten feet from where Joanna sat.

"I've conferred with the lieutenant and ensign," said the officer pontifically. "We've decided 'twould be well to have you play the bagpipes every Muster Day. Mr. Gifford has given his permission. And ye're to wear the kilt you wore to battle. 'Twill look more martial-like."

Ross gave no answer that Joanna could hear. His eyes had a strange look, half pleased, half angered. Obviously the captain expected no reply. He was the chief officer; the piper was but a bondman. He gave the order for the final formation, and Ross sounded the notes of the march.

For a moment Joanna's heart leaped. Would this be

enough to keep Ross here? The thought had scarcely entered her mind before she discarded it. No, it would take more than the playing of the bagpipes once a month to outweigh his dream of escape.

All too soon the afternoon ended. As the sun's rays lengthened, families regrouped, mothers picked up baskets and small garments discarded in the heat of the day, and gathered their broods about them.

The road back seemed longer than in the morning. Was it because she was tired, wondered Joanna, or because Ross walked with a knot of young men, sons of Hammersmith settlers, exchanging sallies in a friendly fashion? They were frank in their admiration, both for his playing of the pipes and for his having fought in the battle of Dunbar. True, Ross had been on the enemy's side, to their way of thinking, but he'd been in the thick of the adventure while they had been dully plowing their fathers' fields.

When they reached the Iron Master's house, Mr. Gifford strode up to the group and tapped Ross on the shoulder. "There's need of another man in the casting shed," he said. "You are to report there for work tomorrow."

Joanna could see Ross's face light up. Now he could learn the secrets of ironmaking. He could find out at first hand how ore and flux and charcoal were transformed into black metal.

"Thank ye, sir," he said. "I'd be well pleased."

The Iron Master entered his house, the group of young men broke up, and Ross started along the road past the Iron Works. He had gone a few steps when he turned back and came up to Joanna standing near the back door.

"Did ye hear that?" he asked, his eyes alight. "I'm to

work in the casting shed, where the hearth is, and the crucible."

"You'll be staying, then?" She hardly dared ask.

"For a time. 'Tis too big a chance to turn away from." He stooped down and picked up his bundle from inside the shed door, where he had thrown it that morning. Then, with a wave of his hand, he was off down the road.

Joanna went into the keeping room and sat down at the table, weak with relief. Until now she hadn't realized how great had been her anxiety. She was sure now that Ross would stay, at least for a while. From the first he'd been fascinated by the Iron Works. She remembered his words the day they arrived: "A man couldna wish to see a grander sight." And the afternoon he had driven her across the snowy fields to the Scots' house. "I'd like well to learn how the iron is made. A body'd find much to admire midst all those machines."

Huldah was emptying the baskets of bits of food. "You can rest *after* supper," she said pointedly.

Joanna got to her feet and began to lay the table. It was warm inside; a little fresh air would be welcome. She threw open a casement, and to her ears came the distant skirl of the pipes, lilting a melody across the rocky hills. It was a merry tune, the one Ross had played the night Maura and Duncan danced. Joanna could feel her pulse quicken, her step lighten. Long after the notes had drifted out of earshot, the song echoed in her mind. Perchance Mr. Whiting was right. Maybe the Lord did have a plan, after all.

17

The Berry Patch

July came, then August. There was news of Indian trouble to the north. On the Contoocook River a man and wife and three children had been slaughtered by savages, and their cabin burned. Some Hammersmith folk spoke of moving to the blockhouse, but no further raids occurred, and the talk died down. Contoocook seemed far away.

Joanna had not dreamed the summer would bring so much activity. She had looked forward to it as a time of leisure, of freedom from the constant fire-making and -tending. But even with Eliza Butt to help, she and Huldah needed every hour of the day.

There were tubs of washing for them to suds and rinse and spread to dry, always with an eye on the great furnace lest the wind shift and scatter sparks and soot over the clean linen. The vegetable garden flourished, seeming full at once of peas to shell, carrots to scrape, and beans to string in the pod and dry in long festoons for winter use.

Raspberries ripened in the hollows. Often Joanna forced

her way through the brambles to garner the crimson globes. Later, blackberries ripened. One morning Ross appeared at the back door with Duncan, who announced he'd been assigned to the casting shed also, though he liked it less than woodcutting. Thrust through his belt was his ax, which he'd brought along to sharpen at the grinding wheel.

The two had brought a message from Maura. She had found a thicket of blackberries between the Scots' house and the Iron Works, with berries enough for an army. Perhaps Joanna would join her there at an hour past noon; 'twas just halfway along the road.

Mistress Gifford was willing, and Joanna set off the minute the midday meal was cleared away. She wore old gloves and a workman's heavy smock, its long sleeves tied down to her wrists. Thus protected, she might save herself from the thorns.

Maura was waiting for her, sitting in the shade of a young birch, watching Hiram and Phineas play with the puppy.

" 'Tis not much work we'll get from the two of them," she said ruefully. Her smile belied her words. She was as fond of the pup as her sons were.

Joanna sat down on the grass and cuddled the little dog for a minute. He wriggled and nibbled at her fingers, giving tiny growls.

"I'm training him. See?" Phineas placed the puppy on the ground and let him frisk for a moment. Then he addressed him with gentle authority. "Sit. Sit, Tip. Sit, I say."

The small beast stood still, then let his hindquarters sink to the ground.

Phineas knelt and caressed him. "Isn't he smart?"

"Wondrously so," agreed Joanna. "Can he shake hands?"

"Not yet," admitted Phineas solemnly. "But he soon will."

"This is pleasant enough, but 'tis not getting us many berries," said Maura. "Phineas, you tie up Tip, and let's all begin picking."

Phineas took some twine from his pocket and knotted a little harness about the dog's body. He fastened one end of the twine to the birch trunk, giving the pup a farewell pat and admonishing him, "You be good now, till I come back."

The berries hung in heavy clusters, ripe and ready to fall at a touch. Farther and farther into the thicket Joanna went. As she stepped among the bushes, parting the tall canes, she could hear Maura's voice and the boys', though she could catch no glimpse of them. She might have been in a separate world of green leaves and blackberries.

How long she picked, she hardly knew, but after a time she realized that the sunshine was losing its warmth and it must be late afternoon. She took up her basket, brimful and heavy, and began to make her way among the thorny bushes.

She had gone only a short distance when she heard Phineas's voice in a scream of terror. "A bear! It's after Tip!"

A bear? Joanna's heart pounded with fear. But she fought her panic. She must try to get to Phineas before the bear turned on him!

Afterward she wondered why she had not simply dropped the heavy basket of berries. As it was, she clutched it tight in her arms to shield her face from the snatching thorns as she tore her way through the bushes in terrified haste. The ground was soft and uneven and strewn with trampled canes. She dared not stumble and fall!

At last she broke out of the thicket. In the open space under the birch the puppy stood shivering at the end of the cord, his tiny tail tight between his legs, pulling back as far as he could from the great brown beast that advanced upon him.

The bear seemed in no hurry. It paused, raked a cluster of berries from a bush, and licked them up with a purple tongue curling out from yellow fangs. Then it fixed its small beady eyes upon the trembling pup and began to lumber toward him.

Off to one side stood Maura, her arms about Phineas, her face chalk-white. She stood rooted as if in a trance. Suddenly Phineas wrenched himself from her grasp, and quick as light he streaked across the clearing and scooped the young dog into his arms. In frantic haste he picked at the twine, trying to unfasten it.

"No, Phineas, let Tip go!" screamed Maura. She lifted her skirts and ran to him, pulling on him in terror. The bear raised up on its haunches.

Joanna could hardly breathe. If only she had a gun, some weapon, perhaps she could fight the beast, at least scare it off. Suddenly she became aware of the basket of berries in her arms. Almost without thinking, she broke into a run, raising it as high as she could, and hurled it with all her force at the bear. The basket struck the beast on the side of its head, emptying a cascade of purple berries over the great body. It staggered momentarily, then with ponderous deliberation dropped to all fours and began to snuff up the fruit.

Beside the birch, Maura still clung to Phineas, the pup clutched to his breast. With his free hand he worked at the knot that fastened Tip's harness to the trunk. Suddenly it parted and, gasping with fright, Maura drew him behind the tree, toward the road.

Alerted by their movement, the bear left the berries and lumbered toward them. It reared up again, a threatening mass of fur and claws, jaws dripping purple juice. Then a sandy-haired man ran up from behind, ax in hand, and sank its blade into the animal's skull!

For a moment the bear stood poised in mid-air, then toppled into a grotesque heap. Maura sank down on the grass, Phineas in her arms, and began to weep hysterically. Hiram ran out from the berry patch where he had been hiding and tried to comfort her.

Only Duncan Muir seemed calm. He surveyed the bear with a calculating eye. "His skin will make a fine rug for the hearth, eh, Maura?" Then he went over to her and somehow managed to encircle them all—woman, boys, and dog—in his strong arms.

Though there were no blackberries that night on the Gifford table, there was excitement over the tale of the brown bear. Soon all Hammersmith resounded with the story of the Scot who had felled a huge bear with one stroke of his ax.

The next day Mr. Gifford unbent from his customary aloofness to compliment Duncan. Duncan took the occasion to remark that he would rather wield an ax any day than pour iron. Afterward, he said he prospered more on the day he killed the bear than on any other. He'd got himself a fine bearskin, got his fellow Scots more fresh meat than they could eat, and he'd regained the work he

liked best, woodcutting. He made no mention of young
Phineas and Tip, or of Maura, but, from the way his eyes
lit up when he looked at any of them, it was clear he considered them more than prize enough. Of another result
of that day's work he was as yet unaware.

For days Joanna was content to stay near the house.
Her taste for berrying had left her the moment she threw
her basket at the bear's head.

Dame Forrest's loom now stood empty. Under her
direction Joanna had finished the coverlet, and it lay
folded neatly in the carved chest, ready against the time
when Debby should have a bed large enough for it.

Each time Joanna stepped into the room, the loom's
empty rollers and heddles mocked her. Finally she gathered up her courage and told the dame of her wish to
weave a tartan for Ross.

Dame Forrest's eyes lit up. "The piper, eh? He seems a
fine upstanding young man. And skillful in casting iron,
so my son-in-law says."

Joanna felt a glow of pride. If the Iron Master had
mentioned his work at home, Ross must be doing well.

"If you bring me the tartan you wish to copy," said
Dame Forrest, "I could tell you how to set up the colors
on the loom. Then you could follow the pattern."

Borrowing the tartan was simple. Joanna spoke to Maura
on the Sabbath, and the following day Maura, unbe-
knownst to Ross, brought the plaid and the skeins of red
wool she had dyed as a surprise for Joanna.

Soon the loom was threaded with dark blue, green,
yellow, and red. Joanna could hardly wait to see the
fabric grow under her fingers. When she could take time
from her other duties, she climbed to the dame's bed-

chamber and seated herself at the loom, delighting in each thrust of the shuttle.

Dame Forrest was a hard teacher. She would brook no shoddy craftsmanship, no slipshod work. Though her hands were knotted, there was nothing wrong with her sight, and she kept an ever-watchful eye upon Joanna and the growing length of tartan. Time and again she insisted that the girl undo a section.

"If 'tis not right now, 'twill never be," she contended. "And you'll never be satisfied with it."

So, painstakingly, Joanna wove the plaid. And into it she wove her dreams and hopes for the future.

18

The Rock Mine

"Tomorrow I'm going to the rock mine at Nahant when the shallop goes for a load of gabbro. If you'd care to come along, you'd be welcome," said the Iron Master to his wife one evening as Joanna was clearing the table.

"May I go, too? And may I invite the Whiting girls?" begged Debby.

"Ask the whole family, if you wish. There'll be room enough."

An hour after sunup the next day, a festive party assembled at the Iron Works wharf. Besides the three little girls, there were Mistress Whiting and Yaweta, as well as the Giffords and Joanna. Soon the shallop was sailing briskly down the Saugus River, past Rumney Marsh and out into the harbor. Joanna sat in the bow with Yaweta. Each held fast to the skirts of the younger girls, who were far too excited to sit quietly. Debby kept leaning over the rail, holding her hands out toward the waves that splashed against the hull.

"Have you ever been to Nahant?" Joanna asked Yaweta.

"Oh, yes. My people go there to fish. They stay for many days and smoke the fish." Yaweta's eyes brightened. "Perchance Indians will be there today." Her dark hair blew back from the beaded band; her crimson scarf fluttered.

The shallop sailed past the long stretch of sand that linked Little and Big Nahant with the mainland. It rounded the farthest point, entered an inlet between two promontories, and drew alongside a rough wharf made of stone blocks.

Two workmen clambered over the rocks to meet them, obviously flustered. It wasn't every day the Iron Master came out to the mine.

"Would you ladies like to see where we get the gabbro?" Mr. Gifford invited.

Ever since he had mentioned gabbro, Joanna had been wondering what it could be. Eagerly she followed Mistress Gifford, holding Debby's hand firmly as they climbed a rough path to the top of a cliff. Soon they came to a quarry where great chunks of rock were strewn about. Here the shoreline was formed of dark igneous rock rising in cliff-like structure. At the base the sea rose and fell in deep swells, now and then foaming into waves.

"Here you see the rock mine. The men loosen the gabbro with bars and picks. Ofttimes they build fires to crack the rock. They trundle it to the boat in those barrows." Mr. Gifford pointed to two squat wheelbarrows filled with chunks of rock. So far as Joanna could see, gabbro looked little different from any other rock she'd seen around Hammersmith.

"Why must you go to all the trouble to fetch rock from here?" asked Mistress Whiting. "Is there none nearer?"

"None to suit the purpose. Gabbro makes a good flux to bring out the impurities in the ore. Until we hit upon this, we used limestone. But that was harder to come by."

"I've never understood what happens when all those sticks and stones get mixed up together in the furnace. I'm almost ready to agree with the Indians that you have a magic power to produce iron," said Mistress Whiting, her eyes dancing.

"Magic—fiddlesticks!" scoffed the Iron Master, though it was clear he was pleased. "It's just a matter of the right proportions of ore, charcoal, and flux. And of course there must be a blast of forced air to bring the fire to sufficient heat."

Joanna listened eagerly.

"The charcoal burns; it melts the ore and gabbro. The gabbro mixes with the impurities in the ore to form slag. And the molten iron drips down into the crucible."

So that was what happened in the great furnace! The bubbling, seething, fiery mass she had seen was molten iron. No wonder Ross was fascinated by the process. She could imagine him working in the hot, gloomy casting shed. If only he could be here on this sparkling, windswept shore.

Debby was pulling at her hand. "I want to go down to the beach," she begged, pointing to a sweeping arc of sand. Joanna shaded her eyes. Were there people moving about at the farther end? And could those be canoes just offshore?

One of the workmen spoke. "Injuns been fishin' there two, mebbe three days."

"Indians?" Mistress Gifford's voice faltered in alarm.

"Please, Mamma, may I go down to play on the sand?" Debby repeated.

"Not with savages nearby," said her mother firmly. "I've heard too many tales of white children being carried off."

Joanna stole a glance at Yaweta. How did she feel, hearing Mistress Gifford express such fears? Apparently unmoved, the girl was looking intently at the group on the other end of the beach. "They are my people," she said with confidence. "They will do no harm."

"If the girls stay at this end, they should be safe enough," said the Iron Master equably.

Down over the rocks Debby and the Whiting girls ran, with Joanna and Yaweta following. Soon they were exploring the waterside. Small pools of clear green water held forests of seaweed, armies of periwinkles and mussels. Horseshoe crabs scuttled for cover. Starfish waved pink arms. The girls took off their shoes and stockings and waded and danced in the waves.

Yaweta had been looking toward the Indians. Now she pointed to a canoe headed in their direction, propelled through the water with powerful strokes by a young man.

"It is Anoka," said Yaweta, a smile lighting her face.

Soon the Indian had nosed his craft onto the sand. It was made of a log, pointed at both ends, and hollowed out. The paddle was decorated with a design in red and black. Anoka leaped out and spoke to Yaweta in the guttural tribal dialect. He was naked save for a loincloth, his tawny skin gleaming in the sunlight, his muscles rippling.

Yaweta drew back and looked toward the hilltop where the two women sat in the shade of a broad oak. "Anoka has asked me to go fishing," she explained. "I do not think I should leave the girls."

"Why not ask Mistress Whiting?" suggested Joanna. "I'll look after the girls." She would have liked nothing better herself than to go out in the small craft, bouncing over the waves.

Yaweta darted up the hill and in a moment returned, joy in every quick footstep. "It is all right. I may go," she said.

Together she and Anoka pushed the craft into deeper water. In one swift movement Yaweta jumped into the bow. A few more steps, and Anoka climbed into the stern and took up his paddle. Its deep strokes thrust the log vessel rapidly out into the bay.

Poised in the bow like a bronze figurehead, Yaweta seemed almost a part of the canoe as it rode the waves. Her face was lifted, her dark hair shone as it blew back from her bright headband. She seemed a different person from the shy, hesitant creature of the Whiting household.

This is where Yaweta belongs, thought Joanna. Here, with her own people, in her own setting—and with Anoka.

She watched the Indian girl drop a baited line over the side, and almost at once pull in a wriggling fish. Anoka put his paddle aside and fished also. Hand over hand, they pulled in many fish.

"Let's play hopscotch," cried Debby. The girls drew outlines with shells in the flat damp sand near the water, threw pebbles into each square, and hopped on one foot to retrieve them. Then there were sand castles to build.

Soon the canoe scraped upon the sand again. Anoka placed haddock, mackerel, and ocean perch near the castles. He handed his knife to Yaweta, who slit and gutted the fish and threw the scraps into the water for the seagulls that flapped and screamed overhead. Then, with a few words of farewell, Anoka shoved the dugout into the water and paddled away.

The fish, broiled on sticks over a fire, made a delicious accompaniment to the picnic lunch.

All too soon the day ended. It seemed to Joanna that one minute they had been stepping ashore at Nahant, the next they were climbing aboard again, sunburned and weary.

The shallop, heavily laden with gabbro, rode low in the water on the return trip, and the wind was less brisk than in the morning. They had covered half the distance between Nahant and the Saugus River when Mr. Gifford pointed out a square-rigged ship anchored off the mouth of the river. It had a dark, gloomy look, and Joanna had a vague feeling of uneasiness as she watched it. A boat was lowered over the side, looking no larger than a pea pod in the distance. Oarsmen rowed the craft up the river, where it was soon lost to sight. The ship, with a spread of dirty, stained canvas, sailed southward down the coast.

Mr. Gifford questioned the steersman of the shallop, but he could recollect only faintly having seen the ship before. He saw so many vessels each time he went to Boston, he said, that he couldn't rightly remember them all. It was strange, he agreed, for a ship to leave a boatful of men behind.

"We'd best keep an eye on the skiff," said Mr. Gifford. But though they searched for another glimpse of the mysterious craft all the way up the river's winding course, they saw no more of it.

"I like not these unauthorized landings," said the Iron Master darkly. "An honest trader would sail directly to a town wharf, or to the Iron Works."

"Think you they might be pirates?" inquired his wife nervously.

"I heard a rumor but yesterday of four men wanted for piracy," he said. "But do not trouble yourself about these men. They may be sailors going home for a night or two."

Despite her husband's reassurance, Mistress Gifford looked nervously about. The day's carefree gaiety was lost.

When they drew alongside the Iron Works wharf, all thoughts of the strange ship were driven away. Mr. Whiting stood waiting for them, surrounded by a group of men and women. From their anxious demeanor, it was evident that something was amiss.

All eyes focused on Yaweta. The minister took her hand as she stepped ashore and said, "You are returning to sorrowful tidings."

She raised a questioning face to his.

"Your father, my child—he has gone to his heavenly reward."

"What has happened to my father?" she asked falteringly.

"I found him early this afternoon when I went to his house to pray with him. He had been dead for several hours."

"Dead? How did he die? He was well on the Sabbath."

The minister shook his head. "I am no physician, but I would guess that he had been poisoned. There was a bowl of corn and beans nearby. It had a strange, unnatural odor."

Yaweta bowed her head and covered her face with her hands. Joanna put a tentative arm about her shoulders.

She could understand only too well the shock of a father's loss. When Yaweta lifted her head and gently dislodged Joanna's arm, she could understand that too. Hadn't she herself feared sympathy?

She watched admiringly as Yaweta lifted her chin and said to Mr. Whiting, "I would like to see my father."

The Whitings and the Indian girl led the way up the hill to the village. Behind them Mistress Gifford and Joanna urged the three little girls along. At the rear, Hammersmith folk crowded about the Iron Master, many talking at once. It was clear that they felt no sorrow at Wapaket's death. It was also clear that they suspected some white man had brought about his death. Who wouldn't want him out of the way, Bible-quoting nuisance that he was? They'd no blame for the man who'd done the evil deed, but they were fearful of what the Indians might do in reprisal. In Ipswich and Haverhill there'd been attacks for less provocation. Hadn't they better all go to the blockhouse, at least for a short time?

Wapaket's burial was conducted with stark brevity. In a hastily fashioned coffin, the Indian's body was lowered into a grave in the churchyard. There was no reading of the scripture, no prayer, and there were few mourners— only the bereaved Yaweta, Joanna, and the Whitings.

As the gravedigger began to fill in the gaping hole, Mistress Whiting tried to draw Yaweta away. But she stood firm until the last shovelful of earth had been thrown in place and packed down. Then, putting her hand on her heart in a gesture of farewell, she stood silently at the foot of the grave. Soon she turned and walked from the cemetery, stiffly erect, her need to be alone apparent to all. Wordlessly they followed her to the Whitings' house.

19

The Blockhouse

The next forenoon a man who'd come from Salem to buy bundles of iron rods announced that there had been an Indian attack on the Chebacco. Bands of warriors had been seen heading southward. It was likely they might stir up the braves hereabouts.

His report strengthened the fear occasioned by Wapaket's poisoning. Hammersmith folk were certain the local savages would strike as soon as the warrior bands arrived. That afternoon settlers and ironworkers toiled over the trail to the blockhouse, a mile from the village.

Family groups straggled along, driving a cow, a few pigs, or a sheep. Men trundled possessions in barrows, with a child or two perched on top. Women carried babies, and perhaps a sack of food or clothing thrown over a shoulder. The few who owned horses loaded them down with necessaries.

The Giffords piled their belongings into one of the wagons used for carting wood. Dame Forrest was seated in a chair in the wagon bed, looking for all the world like an aged queen enthroned. Heaped about her feet were sacks of meal and vegetables, blankets and clothing, pots and pans.

Beside the wagon walked Mistress Gifford, Debby, Joanna, and Huldah, who was none too happy at leaving her precious keeping room. Mr. Gifford had decided he could not abandon the Iron Works. He had collected all the weapons that could be spared from the watchhouse and was organizing volunteer worker-defenders into squads for working and standing sentry duty.

Driving the wagon was Ross, chosen from among those who had elected to remain at the Iron Works. He held the horse to a slow pace so that Dame Forrest might not be jolted unnecessarily. Even so, her chair wobbled alarmingly, and Mistress Gifford asked Joanna to climb into the wagon and hold it steady. Braced against the sideboards, she kept fast hold of the chair and talked with Ross.

Despite the imminence of an Indian attack, he could speak of nothing but ironmaking. Of course he had volunteered to stay and work. There were orders to fill—for iron bars, for kettles, and for firebacks, iron plates to be set into the backs of fireplaces, where the heat was most intense. He'd made a design for a special fireback for a settler named Seth Rountree. He'd put a round tree in the center, with an S for *Seth* in one corner, an A for his wife *Ann* in the other, and an R at the bottom. Seth was delighted with the idea. Ross was working on a design for another fireback, he said mysteriously, but it would not be needed for a while yet.

Trailing behind the Giffords came Maura, Hiram, and Duncan Muir, carrying a tearful Phineas on his shoulder.

They were late, Maura explained, because Phineas had not been able to find his dog. One minute Tip was there; the next he had disappeared. Phineas was sure an Indian had caught him and would make him into stew.

"Ye shouldna be worrit," Duncan soothed the boy. "Ye ken full well he's aye chasin' after the rabbits. I'll bring him to ye myself as soon as I can."

At the entrance to the watchhouse Duncan set Phineas on the ground, laid a fond hand on his head, and said farewell to Maura. He and Ross must hasten back to the Iron Works before dark if they didn't want to be mistaken for savages and get bullets in their skulls from the sentries' muskets. Though he laughed, there was no mistaking the seriousness of his tone.

Ross drove the wagon into the stockade and helped unload it. He and Duncan lifted Dame Forrest and her chair onto the ground. Then they left.

Joanna watched them go along the track to Hammersmith, thankful that Ross and Duncan would be together. They had fought side by side at Dunbar. If need be, they would fight side by side at Hammersmith. She prayed they would both come through unscathed.

For the space of two or three acres around the blockhouse the ground had been cleared so that no savages could creep up unseen. Joanna looked in the direction of the Iron Works. The trees hid the settlement, but in the sky glowed the red light of the furnace's great flame. She could feel an answering glow in her heart. Somewhere near that fire Ross would be working. Just knowing he was there was comforting.

The Whiting family was grouped near the entrance of the stockade. The minister greeted people as they came in, attempting to soothe their fears. Mistress Whiting spoke to the wives and children, cheering them with words of comfort.

As evening fell, Joanna found Yaweta in a shadowy corner of the stockade, her body pressed against the log piles, her face buried in her hands. She looked up, at Joanna's approach, her eyes bleak with sorrow.

Joanna pondered. What could she say? What words could she speak that would help Yaweta through her grief? She put her hand on the Indian girl's. "I can understand somewhat how you feel," she said. "My father died on the ship coming to this land."

Yaweta's dark eyes, filled with melancholy, were fixed on Joanna. But she said not a word.

"You can visit your father's grave," continued Joanna. "Mine was buried at sea."

Yaweta shuddered. Still she said nothing.

"At least your father was buried in the churchyard," Joanna went on. "That would have pleased him."

"But he has no food to eat on his journey to the land of the Great Spirit. He has no weapons to protect him on the way."

Joanna was on the point of saying that in heaven Wapaket would have no need of food and weapons. Then she recalled the grave at the rim of the Indian village, seeing the baskets and bow as clearly as if they were before her.

"How can I honor my father, as the Bible says, if I do not help him on his last journey?" pursued Yaweta.

"You can pray for him," said Joanna. "I will pray with you if you wish."

In the darkness the two girls bowed their heads. For long minutes they prayed in silence.

As Joanna lifted her eyes, she saw with alarm that a group of excited men and women were approaching, their voices a babble of ugly sound. Some bore flaming pine knots. Others raised their arms in threatening gestures. They drew nearer, their voices loud.

"There's the Indian girl now, hiding in the corner."

"She don't belong in the stockade with us folks."

"Let's put her out of here!"

Joanna searched the hostile faces. Were these the God-fearing people of Hammersmith, these angry, frightened creatures? Obadiah Talbot towered in the front rank like an avenging fury. In the middle of the crowd was his wife, her face red as a turkey cock's, and beside her Huldah, the embodiment of righteous wrath.

Thrusting Yaweta back into the corner, Joanna stood squarely in front of her and faced the angry mob.

"What do you want?"' she demanded. "Yaweta has done no harm to you." Her voice sounded shrill and high in her ears.

"Her being here is wrong!" called out Goody Talbot. "Why don't she stay where she belongs, with the other savages?"

"She'll open the gates and let the Indians in!"

"She'll kill us in our sleep!"

"She'll want revenge for her father's murder!"

The cries resounded with hatred. How could these people be so stupid? Joanna could feel her choler rising.

"Yaweta is our friend," she shouted as loudly as she could. But her words were drowned in the tumult of the crowd.

"Put her out! Put her out!" The words were repeated again and again.

The crowd advanced. Joanna could hear the torches crackling and could feel their heat on her face. Obadiah Talbot stepped forward and put a hand on Joanna's arm.

"Stand back," he ordered. "Let me get hold of that Indian."

Joanna tried to shake off his grip. It was like iron. She clawed at his arm with her other hand. She might have been trying to dislodge the limb of a tree. Frantic, she bent her head and sank her teeth into his wrist. It was all bone and sinew, but she put her utmost strength into the bite until she tasted blood.

"Augh!" Obadiah Talbot shook his hand free and struck Joanna on the side of the head. The blow sent her reeling. As she fell against Yaweta, she heard as from a distance the voice of Mr. Whiting, usually mild, now thundering in anger.

"You must not harm the Indian maid. Have you no compassion on the fatherless?"

He stood in front of the girls, both arms raised. His white beard and hair shone in the torchlight. So must the prophets of old have looked, thought Joanna. For all he had a slight, almost frail form, he seemed to be invested with a supernatural strength. The mob fell back, muttering.

Obadiah Talbot alone stood his ground stubbornly, one hand cupped about his injured wrist. "We're none of us safe while she's inside the stockade. If we stay here, we may be slaughtered through her treachery."

"Yaweta would no more betray us than I would myself,"

declared Mr. Whiting passionately. "I give you my word she will be true to us."

He put one arm about Yaweta's shoulders, facing the angry crowd. "Go back to your families," he commanded, "and pray to the Lord for forgiveness. If you truly repent, He may stay His hand from full vengeance."

Her head swimming, Joanna followed the minister and Yaweta to the space shared by the Giffords and Whitings, and stretched out on a blanket next to Debby. There was a rustle in the straw beside her, and Yaweta lay down. Joanna reached out in the darkness and took the Indian girl's hand. She could feel it shaking. How she longed to speak some word of comfort! But the blockhouse had become silent. Now was no time to talk, with most of the village gathered under this one roof, listening with tense ears for any alien sound. She would have to wait until morning.

The next morning, alas, was too late. When Joanna awoke at dawn, itching from the straw that had poked through the blanket and her clothing, she saw at once that Yaweta's place was empty. Where she had lain was now only a neatly folded blanket.

Like a deluge of icy water, realization swept over Joanna. Poor Yaweta! Last night had been too much. She could not remain here, surrounded by those who hated and feared her. Small wonder she had fled.

Unaware of Yaweta's departure, the Whitings slept peacefully. The minister's white beard rose and fell on his chest. The little girls lay quiet as dolls, their mother composed. Next to Joanna, Debby tossed restlessly, and

Dame Forrest snored gustily. Even Mistress Gifford was deep in heavy slumber.

Where had Yaweta gone? Without warning a picture of the Pequot woman flashed across Joanna's mind. Once more she saw the leap into the harbor, heard the doleful scream. Terror struck her. Would Yaweta take a similar course? What she had suffered could be provocation enough—first the killing of Wapaket, then the threats of the mob. In two days she had lost not only her father but quite possibly her belief in the faith he had espoused so completely.

Perhaps, if she hurried, she might find Yaweta. Quickly Joanna wakened Mr. Whiting, then ran out of the crowded building into the stockade. Anxiously she looked about for some sign of the Indian girl. A few women straggled toward an open hogshead of water that stood in a muddy puddle with flies and hornets circling above. Yaweta was not with the women. Men were coming and going through the wide gates, taking stock out to graze in nearby fields. Two guards stood beside the entrance, chaffing with the men driving cattle. No, they had not seen Yaweta.

Joanna had started out through the gate when she felt a heavy hand on her shoulder. "And where might ye be going?" inquired the guard. "My orders is to keep all women and children inside." His eyes were red-rimmed above unshaven cheeks.

"Please let me go," implored Joanna. "I must find Yaweta." She was almost weeping in her anxiety. Couldn't the men understand it was a matter of life and death?

"Orders is orders," said the guard firmly. "You stay inside." He gave her a shove in the direction of the blockhouse.

Mr. Whiting was in the courtyard. He too was distressed. "Three years' work gone, wiped out in a single day, just as I had hopes of a goodly harvest of souls. Why can I not bring Christ to these heathen as do others of my brethren in the ministry?" He pressed a hand against his forehead. "Has anyone seen her?" he asked Joanna.

"No one," she answered sorrowfully. Should she confide in him her fear of what Yaweta might do? She was about to speak when Mr. Whiting said, "Be not afraid. The Lord is with Yaweta. Surely He will protect her."

He paused a moment, then added in a matter-of-fact tone, "She has probably gone to her mother. This was the day of her regular visit." A smile brightened his face. "Of course. That is the answer. She has gone to see her mother. Surely she will return at nightfall, as is her custom."

No one but Joanna seemed to be disturbed at Yaweta's absence. Joanna marveled at others' calm acceptance of Mr. Whiting's explanation. She herself was consumed with anxiety. Why had Yaweta stolen away without a word? She must have feared that someone would try to stop her.

The day dragged on. As the sun rose higher, the heat within the blockhouse became stifling. The stockade, with its scant shade, was like an oven, its high wall a barrier to every breeze. Joanna sat between Debby and the Whiting girls, drawing pictures for them in the dust.

At sundown there came a cry from a guard posted at a lookout station at one corner of the stockade fence.

"Indians!"

Men rushed about, loading muskets, taking up positions at loopholes. A number stationed themselves near the gate. Others filled fire buckets in case the savages should set fire to the blockhouse with flaming arrows.

The guard called out again. "There be just two. One is a woman, and the man is not armed."

The commanding officer strode through the courtyard. "Hold your fire," he ordered, and climbed to the lookout post. His voice rang out loud and clear. "Why come you here?"

"To talk with the white-bearded one."

Mr. Whiting stepped forward. "That's what the Indians call me," he said. "Will you let them in?"

The officer hesitated. "I'd best not," he said. "I can see only two savages, but it might be a ruse."

Joanna peered through a space between two logs. At first she could see only the dry grass of the cleared area outside. Then she made out two figures at the edge of the forest. One was Anoka, and the other—surely it could be no one but Yaweta's mother.

In a moment she had told Mr. Whiting. At his insistence the gates were opened a crack and he slid outside. Joanna could see him crossing the open area with a wary, though deliberate step, to the two Indians.

Their voices were low; she could not hear their words. For long minutes they talked; then Mr. Whiting returned to the stockade, his step slow, his hands hanging listlessly.

"They came for Yaweta," he said as he entered. "They thought she was here." He wore a stricken look.

An icy fear gripped Joanna. She had known all along that Yaweta was in danger. She might have intended to go to the Indian village when she left the stockade, but some dreadful accident had prevented her from arriving there. Had she lost her way as she traveled through the night, grief-stricken and exhausted? Might she have stumbled into the swamp? Could she have been attacked by wild beasts? Joanna felt her skin prickle at the memory of the monster bear at the berry patch. In the darkness such a creature might have killed Yaweta.

Then her mind cleared, and suddenly she knew, as positively as if she had heard the words spoken, that Yaweta was in *mortal* danger. In the same moment she knew that it was her duty to find Yaweta and save her from whatever threatened.

20

The Pirates' Glen

Getting out of the blockhouse was a simple matter. Joanna waited until dusk, when herdsmen returned, driving cattle before them. Crouching low, she slipped out the open gate as a drove of cows entered. Then she circled, unseen, to the rear of the stockade, keeping close to its high wall, and crept away in the shadows to the cover of the woods.

Conjecturing that Yaweta would go either to her father's house or to find Anoka in Nahant, Joanna had planned her route carefully. First she would go to Wapaket's hut, a mile or so beyond the Scots' house on the way to the Indian village. If she found no sign of Yaweta there, she would go to the Saugus River near the Iron Works, where many small craft were tied up. A number of settlers used dugout canoes like the Indians'. It was more than likely that Yaweta would use one of those to get to Nahant.

Dusk swiftly deepened into darkness. Joanna had never

been in the woods at night before. It was incredible that
they could be so black, or that the two miles to the Scots'
house could seem so endless. She proceeded slowly, her
hands stretched out before her, keeping to the path by
feeling the branches on either side. Gradually her eyes became accustomed to the darkness; she could make out dim
shapes of tree trunks.

Now and then she could hear light rustlings in the
leaves. An owl hooted, startling her into frozen im-
mobility. A large shadow loomed before her. Could it be
a bear? She could almost see the yellow fangs and dripping jaws. She broke into a cold sweat, rooted to the
ground. How could she find courage to keep on? She
would have to return to the safety of the blockhouse.

Then Yaweta's face flashed into her mind. She could not
turn back now. She must go on and try to find her. The
path led into a clearing, and thankfully she stepped into
the open space. A full moon, rising, showed the outline of
the Scots' house. She felt a surge of gratitude at the
familiar sight.

The door, swinging on its hinges, creaked eerily. A
breeze opened it wide, and a shaft of moonlight lit the
room and fell across the table. Were those Ross's bagpipes
lying there? She went in, glancing fearfully into the dark
corners. How strange the room seemed with no firelight
and no friendly voices! Ross had once asked her to keep
the bagpipes safe for him. She'd not leave them here for
a marauding band of Indians. Snatching them up, she ran
out the door and into the moonlit yard.

Suddenly a furry form launched itself at her feet. She
nearly flew back into the house. Then came a high, welcoming bark. Tip! She bent down and caressed the dog,

thankful for his presence. Perhaps now she would not be so fearful.

She had crossed the clearing and was about to enter the woods to continue on her way to Wapaket's hut when a tall form blocked her path. She could make out a silhouette that was unmistakably Indian, from the fringed leggings to the feather in the hair. Terror gripped her; a scream rose in her throat. Then a voice spoke.

"Do not fear. It is Anoka."

She could only gasp with relief.

"Why is white girl not in blockhouse?"

"I am searching for Yaweta." She told him her plan.

He listened gravely and said, "Anoka go Wapaket's house today. Yaweta there before. Gone now. Maybe at river. We look."

He stepped ahead of her and with swift, silent tread led the way across the clearing and down the road to the Iron Works. Joanna followed, hurrying to keep up, thankful that she need not go to Wapaket's hut. It was bad enough to be in the dark woods. At least she did not have to travel this mile alone. Behind her Tip padded along, quiet after his first shrill outburst.

Their way led past the meetinghouse and burying ground, now flooded with full moonlight. Was it only two days ago that Wapaket had been buried here? Joanna looked toward the grave, then rubbed her eyes and looked again. On the freshly heaped mound lay several small baskets and a bow and arrow. She reached out and touched Anoka's arm and pointed to the grave.

"Yaweta bring food and arrows for father," he said gravely. "A good daughter."

The red glow from the furnace lighted the sky. As they drew near to the Iron Works it grew brighter, and they could see figures working near the stack. Noiselessly they made their way to a thicket near the edge of the open space surrounding the furnace. A sentry with musket over his shoulder paced toward them, a black and white dog at his side.

Anoka gave a sibilant hiss, then said in a low tone, "Ross."

The Scot, his musket at the ready, advanced toward the trees. "Who is it?" he asked.

The dog, growling, stalked toward them on stiff legs. Tip bounded forward, barking. A minute later Ross put his weapon down and greeted Anoka, as Joanna emerged from the shadows and quieted the dogs. Then she and the two young men held a whispered conference.

Ross would ask Duncan to stand his watch while he and Anoka continued the search for Yaweta. Joanna had best remain at the Iron Works, where she would be safe.

Joanna's temper flared. Had she gone through the terrors of the night only to be shut up in the Iron Works while Ross and Anoka carried out her plan?

She stamped her foot. "I'll not remain here," she said vehemently. "I'm going with you, whether you like it or not."

In the moonlight she could see the amazement on Ross's face. "If that is the way ye feel, come ahead, then," he said. "I guess we canna stop ye." Was she imagining it, or was there admiration in his tone?

It took but a moment for Ross to rout out Duncan. He shook his head dourly at their plan but agreed to take

Ross's turn as sentry. Stooping, he picked up Tip, muttering, "This one'll be nae help to ye."

Anoka, Ross, and Joanna made their way toward the wharf, keeping to the shadows of the buildings. As they went past the forge, Ross gave a low whistle of surprise. A piece of foolscap tacked to the door fluttered in the breeze. He peered at the paper, held it to the moonlight, and read in a low voice: "Make four sets of manacles and two sets of leg irons. Will call for same one month hence. A. Leach."

Ross stood for a moment in silence. " 'Tis odd that Leach left a note instead of coming himself as before. Mayhap he saw the sentries with their muskets and feared to be challenged."

He turned to Joanna. "It's just come to me. Was Leach not the captain of the ship the Indian woman jumped from? And that day he came here to pick up his irons, he asked if there were other Indians about. Do ye recall how he looked at Yaweta?"

Joanna nodded, feeling sick with horror. She was certain now that Yaweta could have fallen into Leach's hands.

Ross explained to Anoka, whose face took on an expression of rage.

"Come now. Find Yaweta," he said urgently.

Ross held the note to Ruff's nose. The dog sniffed at it, whining nervously, his fur rising. "Go find him," Ross ordered. "Find Leach."

Ruff circled about with his nose to the ground. Then with a growl he led the way down the hill and into the woods. He remembers Leach, thought Joanna. He remembers how he hated him. Ruff led them, now and then giving a scarcely audible whine.

Joanna stumbled after the two young men, the bagpipes growing heavier with each step. If only she had left them at the Iron Works. She'd like to put them down now, but in the tangle of underbrush she might never find them again. Better to struggle ahead as best she could.

They had gone perhaps a quarter of a mile when Anoka, in the lead, stooped and picked up something from the pathway. He held it up for the others to see. Joanna gave a gasp of surprise and relief. It was Yaweta's beaded headband, glinting in the moonlight! There was no doubt now that she had come this way. If only there was still time to find her before Leach could do her harm!

Another quarter of a mile and they came to the rim of a deep hollow. Below them a faint light showed, a tiny gleam among the trees. With infinite caution they edged nearer, down the slope, until a huge boulder gave them a place of concealment. At first, peering out, they could see only the flicker of a very small fire. Then they saw two figures sitting near its light. One was cleaning a musket. The other, Abner Leach himself, was puffing on a pipe. At the edge of the shadows lay two other men. Joanna strained her eyes for any sign of Yaweta. At length she saw a slight movement against a birch tree. A head moved, with long hair showing dark against the white tree trunk. It was Yaweta! Thank heaven she was still alive.

"We can surprise them," Ross whispered, "if we work fast."

Anoka muttered in assent. The two young men conferred briefly in almost inaudible voices. Then Ross laid his hand lightly on Joanna's shoulder.

"Stay here where ye'll be safe," he admonished. "Should we fail, ye can run off unseen and escape."

Words came to Joanna's lips and froze there. Anything she might say would sound foolish. She couldn't tell Ross to be careful when he was going into certain, perhaps mortal danger. She was shivering, with cold or fear, or both. Hugging the bagpipes to her, she only nodded her head mutely.

Ross and Anoka melted out of sight into the darkness, Ruff a shadow at their heels. Straining her eyes, she saw them making their way toward the fire, two shadows slipping from tree to tree. Suddenly they seemed very young, scarcely a match for four men used to violence and bloodshed.

Just then a wild screech sounded, and Anoka, brandishing his tomahawk, leaped into the firelight. Another fearsome call rent the air, a Scot's battle cry. Ross lunged into the firelit circle, his musket pointed at Leach and his companions.

"Stand and put up your hands ere I shoot!" ordered Ross.

The man cleaning the musket threw it down and scrambled to his feet. Leach moved more slowly, raising himself with deliberation. Grasping his pipe in one hand, he suddenly threw it straight at Ross's head. The glowing tobacco shot toward his face. Ross ducked, and in the moment he was off guard Leach jumped on him, grabbing the barrel of his musket and trying to force him over backward. The two struggled silently for possession of the weapon. Ruff circled around their feet, snarling and growling, darting back and forth, striving to get a hold on Leach's leg.

The man by the fire picked up the musket he had been cleaning, grasped the barrel in both hands, and brandished it over his head. He was about to bring the stock down on Ross's skull when Anoka struck him on the shoulder with his tomahawk. The man dropped the musket, clapped his hand to the wound, and fell to the ground.

The two men who had been sleeping stumbled to their feet. One pulled a knife from his belt and was raising his arm to hurl it at Ross when Anoka leaped on him, clutching his wrist. The other man threw himself on the Indian, beating him with clenched fists.

Joanna watched in mounting terror. Two young men could not possibly overcome the four pirates! And if they failed, what would happen to Yaweta? Ross and Anoka would probably be killed. Suddenly Joanna was blazing with anger. She couldn't stand here looking on. Surely she could do something!

She reached for a broken branch caught in a crevice of the boulder, thinking she might use it as a weapon. But her hand drew back as inspiration seized her. The bagpipes! Now was the time to play all Ross had taught her, and Leach would think the militia was coming!

Almost suffocated by the wild beating of her heart, Joanna blew air into the sheepskin bag. Now the chanter. Her fingers found the holes. She pressed her elbow against the bag, but only a muffled whine sounded. She could do better than that! Her shaking fingers moved on the chanter, and with a tremendous effort she jammed her elbow hard against the sheepskin. The notes flowed out, sounding to her anxious ears like mere squawks. She must try harder!

What was the tune Ross had taught her, the march that

every piper learned first? Frantically she forced her fingers to remember, and this time they moved with certainty. Her arm pressed rhythmically against the bag. The notes came forth, not as true and strong as Ross might play them, but with unmistakable vigor. Little matter that they were born of fear. They were the notes of a march, a song of battle. Some of their spirit communicated itself to her and lent her courage. Though her lungs were aching with the effort of keeping the bag inflated, she kept on playing.

Through the wail of the pipes she could hear Ross shout, "Best give up, Leach. They're coming!"

"Who's coming?" Leach grunted. He looked over his shoulder in the direction of the piping, and in that instant Ross tore the musket from his grasp and turned its muzzle full upon him.

At the same instant Ruff hurled himself on Anoka's assailant and sank his fangs into the man's forearm. The knife dropped, and Anoka pounced on it.

Still breathing hard from the struggle with Leach, Ross swung his musket to cover the four pirates. He spoke to Anoka, and the Indian moved swiftly to the tree where Yaweta was tied and cut her bonds. Then he whirled and, like a demon of vengeance, bore down on Leach, tomahawk in hand. He held up a lock of the man's hair in his left hand and was about to strike at his scalp when Ross shouted, "No, Anoka! We'll take them alive."

"Better dead," Anoka said bitterly and kept the tomahawk poised, his eyes glinting.

"Better to take them prisoner." Ross's tone was urgent. "Tie them with that rope!"

Anoka lowered the weapon and, while Ross kept them

covered with the rifle, bound the four men's hands securely
with the cords that had fastened Yaweta to the tree.

Holding fast to the bagpipes, which emitted squeals
and squawks with every step she took, Joanna stumbled
into the open space near the fire and hurried to where
Yaweta sat rubbing feeling back into her numbed hands
and feet. If she had been terrified watching the struggle,
how much more fearful must Yaweta have been, bound
hand and foot, knowing that her fate hung in the balance!

"Did they harm you?" she asked the Indian girl, rubbing
at her wrists and ankles where the ropes had cut deeply.

"No," said Yaweta. She seemed dazed with exhaustion,
and her eyes were focused on Anoka, who was bending
over Leach.

Joanna had to know more. "Where did they catch you?"

"Near the river," said Yaweta. "I was looking for a canoe
so I could go to Nahant and tell Anoka about my father."

I was right about that, thought Joanna.

"They meant to take me on their ship across the ocean
and sell me as a slave," continued Yaweta with a shudder.
"I am glad you came," she finished simply.

Joanna was grateful for the darkness. Tears were
streaming down her cheeks, tears of relief and thankful-
ness. She put her arm about Yaweta. "You are safe now,"
she said.

Even as she said the words, her mind raced ahead. How
safe would Yaweta be at the blockhouse? Had she escaped
one peril only to return to another? She could imagine the
hostility of the settlers if Yaweta should return to the
stockade.

Joanna was helping Yaweta to her feet when Ross said,
never lifting his eyes from the pirates, "A fine bit of piping

that was, the most welcome that's e'er come to my ears. 'Twas worth every bit of the trouble it took to teach ye."

"Trouble?" Joanna flared. "I care not if I ever pipe another note." But inwardly she felt a glow of pride at her part in the pirates' capture.

In a short while they set off on the trek back to the Iron Works. Leach and his men were in the lead, cursing and grumbling, their hands tied behind their backs with the same cords that had secured Yaweta to the tree. Behind them stalked Ross and Anoka, weapons ready for action. The two girls followed, Ruff at their heels.

They had made their difficult way through the woods and were approaching the cleared fields near the Iron Works when Anoka spoke over his shoulder.

"Why are white men in blockhouse? What do they fear?"

"They heard that Indians killed a family on the Chebacco River," said Joanna, "and think they may come this way and join with your people to attack Hammersmith."

"My people friend to white men," said Anoka. "We stop Chebacco Indians from hurting white men."

"The Hammersmith folk are afraid of your people because of Wapaket's death," continued Joanna. "They fear the Indians will attack them because white men are likely the ones that killed Wapaket."

There were enough who had hated Wapaket, she thought—Obadiah Talbot, for one, and the man whose son had fallen from the tree while clubbing pigeons on the Sabbath. There must be others too.

Anoka said slowly, "White men have no reason to fear. Indians gave poison to Wapaket. Say if white man's god is powerful, he will save Wapaket from poison. But not so." A minute later he added, "My father, the sachem, will punish them."

Dumfounded, Joanna could say not a word.

Ross, with characteristic matter-of-factness, said only, "Then the people can leave the blockhouse and get back to work."

Beside her, Joanna heard Yaweta murmuring, "My poor father! He meant no harm, but he had many enemies."

And so do you mean no harm, but you have many enemies, thought Joanna, and only because you are of another color, another race, whom few take the trouble to understand or befriend.

At the Iron Works, Ross gave a shout to Duncan, who roused the Iron Master. A group of workmen gathered in minutes. Soon they had locked Leach and his companions in the stout warehouse on the wharf.

Mr. Gifford listened while Ross recounted the night's exploits. "We'll interrogate Leach in the morning," he said. "Methinks he may be the Leach who's wanted for piracy."

He gave Joanna a quizzical gaze. "Meanwhile, what's to be done with these young women? 'Tis unseemly for maids to be out at this hour of the night."

Joanna thought frantically. She dared not take Yaweta back to the blockhouse. Perhaps they might stay at the Iron Master's house? She was about to ask, when Anoka spoke with authority.

"Anoka take Yaweta to mother now."

Yaweta looked up at him gratefully, then turned to Joanna. "You will tell the Whitings I have gone to my home?"

To her home. There was a world of meaning in the

word, and finality. Without asking, Joanna knew that
Yaweta would never return to the Whitings. With her
father dead, she no longer felt obliged to live with the
minister's family. His death had freed her to return to her
own people.

"I will tell them," said Joanna. She embraced Yaweta
and watched her walk away with Anoka. Only two days
ago she had looked at them in the dugout canoe at the
Indian fishing grounds and thought how much more naturally Yaweta fitted into that setting than into the Hammersmith life. She felt the same way now, seeing them
slip away into the darkness.

She had little time for her thoughts. The Iron Master
was studying her face, his gaze intent.

"Even if you could make it on foot to the blockhouse,
which I doubt," he said slowly, "you'd be in danger from
overzealous sentries. They might shoot first and ask your
identity later. You'd best stay here."

"In your house?" quavered Joanna. She could feel her
courage ebbing away at the thought of the dark empty
rooms.

The Iron Master smiled. "No. I'd rather you spent what's
left of the night in the casting shed, where we can keep
an eye on you."

He led the way into the rough-timbered structure that
fanned out from the base of the blast furnace. The great
hearth shone with an intense light, the molten iron seething in the crucible, with drops of liquid fire raining onto
its surface.

A workman who stood at one side of the hearth holding
a long metal rod announced, "It's nigh time for the tap-
ping, sir."

"There's a pallet in the corner where you can rest," said the Iron Master to Joanna.

Rest? When the furnace was about to be tapped? Folk came from miles around to watch that sight. She was weary, but not enough to miss the excitement of seeing the iron poured.

"I'd rather watch, if I may," she said.

"Very well. But stand back out of the way. McCrae, you see to her."

Ross steered Joanna off to one side, midway between the crucible and molds, where she could see clearly. At a signal from Mr. Gifford, the workman knocked the clay plug from the crucible. A fiery stream gushed forth, flowed down a trench dug in the sloping sandy floor, into a long narrow indentation with four others angling off from it. The red-hot metal hissed and sizzled, cooling to a dull gray. The larger space would make a sow bar, explained Ross, the four smaller ones, pigs of iron.

Other workmen took long-handled iron ladles, dipped the molten metal from the crucible, and poured it into molds. Some were for weights, said Ross, some for kettles. Other large flat molds were for firebacks. He spoke again of a fireback he hoped to make in the future. He was carving the wooden mold for it in his spare time. One day he would show it to her.

Joanna watched and listened in fascination, the intense light, the shadowy figures, seeming like a dream. Suddenly the events of the night began to take their toll. Fatigue engulfed her. Gratefully she let Ross lead her to a pallet, sank down upon it, and almost instantly fell into heavy sleep.

21

Days of Decision

The following morning the Iron Master, the magistrate, and the captain of the militia interrogated Leach and his companions. Joanna watched from the window as the four pirates were escorted under guard to the Iron Master's parlor. Earlier she had gone to the house, built up a fire, and made a hot breakfast for Mr. Gifford and the men.

At the sight of Leach's ratlike face, she could not repress a shudder. Unshaven and unkempt, he looked even more odious than she had remembered. What a monster he was to capture and sell Indians as slaves!

The other three men were no more prepossessing. The man whose shoulder had been cut by the tomahawk wore a bloody bandage. He was a stout, beefy fellow, with a sinister twist to his mouth. Another had a soiled kerchief about his head; from one ear dangled a brass earring. The third was extremely thin, with sallow skin and sunken eyes.

The meeting lasted but a short time. The four were

marched back to the warehouse, and a guard posted outside. Workmen gathered about the officials, eager to hear what action would be taken.

Bursting with curiosity, Joanna ran down the hillside. She was in time to hear the magistrate announce, "The men captured last night are Abner Leach and some of his crew. All are wanted for piracy. They will be sent to England for trial, and their ship, the *Hydra*, will be sought. The rowboat they came ashore in will be auctioned off and the proceeds put into town funds."

A shout arose from the crowd. They gathered around Ross, clapping him on the back and praising him.

He protested, saying, " 'Twas not myself alone who caught them. There were others with me." He looked toward Joanna, but she fled up the hill. What she had done was little enough, and that all due to the bagpipes.

From Mr. Gifford she heard later that Ross and Anoka would accompany four members of the militia to Boston with the prisoners. If there was any reward, they would be on hand to receive it. Ross had been sent to find Anoka, and they would set out the next day.

Reward? Soon all Hammersmith was buzzing with rumors. There'd be ten pounds, twenty, perhaps fifty for the capture of such a crew of blackguards. It was monstrous the number of ships Captain Leach had sunk, the innocent people he'd robbed and killed, to say nothing of those he had sold into slavery.

Listening to the talk, Joanna felt her hopes soar. Perhaps Ross would get enough to buy his freedom. There might even be a sum large enough to buy hers too. She'd helped somewhat in the capture. Ross would be sure to share some part of the reward money with her. She'd need only a little more than four pounds, now that nearly a year of her indenture had passed.

During the day weary families streamed out of the blockhouse back to their homes, thankful to be released from the irksome confinement. When the Giffords reached the house, Joanna greeted them at the door, fearful of an expected tongue-lashing for her secret departure during the night.

To her amazement, Mistress Gifford threw her arms about her, exclaiming, "You are safe, God be thanked!"

Debby gave her a sticky kiss, and Dame Forrest said stiffly, "We were distraught about you, child."

Could it be that the Giffords really cared about her? Joanna felt giddy with relief and happiness.

Huldah, coming up the path laden with bundles, jerked her back to reality and her place in the household. "The least you can do is help unload this stuff, after running off and leaving me to do all the packing-up alone."

Only one casualty was reported by those newly arrived from the blockhouse. Obadiah Talbot had been so infuriated when he learned that there was no danger of an Indian attack that he suffered a stroke. All for nothing, he had lost three days of harvest time, he screamed just before the seizure silenced him.

Duncan Muir, who had come to the blockhouse to fetch Maura and the boys, had carried the old man to a pallet on a wagon and helped Goody Talbot to a cushion next to him. He'd driven them to their home, with Maura and the boys on the seat beside him. He'd carried Obadiah into the house, set him on his bed, and not left till he'd brought in wood and water and all their belongings. Then he had bid Maura stay to help, saying he and the other Scots could fend for themselves for a while.

The next day Joanna saw Maura hurrying along the road by the Iron Master's house, her face white and drawn. She was fair done in, she confessed, with waiting on her father-in-law. A more demanding man than Obadiah Talbot there never was. He'd got back the use of his tongue and put all his strength into issuing commands. She was on her way to fetch the magistrate to the old man's bedside. He'd taken it into his head to make a new will. She looked for not a shilling for herself, but she hoped he'd leave something to her boys.

A day later, to the relief of all except his faithful wife, Goodman Talbot died. He'd been hard to live with when well, impossible to put up with when sick. His last will and testament created a furor that lasted for weeks.

He'd made the usual bequests—the house to his widow for her lifetime, with annual supplies of corn, apples, and beef. So many acres went to this son, so many acres to that one.

At the very end he had bequeathed "one bull, one cow, two sheep, all my tools and implements, and the sum of forty pounds to Duncan Muir, the Scot who saved my grandson's life, on the condition that he marry Maura, widow of my deceased son John, and raise her sons in the Christian way."

Joanna could remember Maura saying cheerily, "We'll wait." Now there was no need for them to put off being wed. Duncan could buy his freedom. He could find land and build the house he and Maura had dreamed of. Joanna hoped they'd not go far away. She had a deep fondness for Maura, and for Hiram and Phineas—for Duncan too, though she thought of him always as Ross's friend.

Meanwhile all the village had been waiting eagerly for the return of the young Scot, the Indian, and the four militiamen. Perchance they'd remained in Boston to celebrate getting the reward. It would not be the first time a man had drunk up a prize. Joanna had her own private fears. Would not Ross, with money in his hand, be tempted to return to Scotland? There in his native land he'd be free. He could take up his old life where he'd left it.

The evening of the fourth day a dusty, footsore band entered Hammersmith. Almost immediately they were surrounded by curious friends and acquaintances.

On the fringe of the crowd, Joanna scanned the faces of the travelers. Ah, there was Ross, hot and tired, but back in Hammersmith. She hadn't known her fear of his going was so great until this minute when she saw him here. Nearby stood Anoka, his bronzed face glistening with perspiration. But who was the young boy beside him? Though wearing English clothes, he was unmistakably Indian, with the same high cheekbones, tawny skin, and straight black hair as Anoka. Now and again he darted a glance at the crowd. But the look he gave to Anoka was one of pure worship.

Ross spoke for the group. "Ye'll be glad to hear that Leach and his men are safely in jail awaiting passage to England for trial. Whilst we were in Boston, the *Hydra* came into port and was taken possession of. The ship will be sold and the money put into the colony's treasury."

Impatient cries burst from the crowd.

"How much reward did you get?"

"What will you do with the money?"

Ross held up both hands for silence. "There was no reward money for Leach's capture," he said, "but the Governor himself received us and gave us a letter of thanks."
He held up a folded parchment.

"A letter?"

"Is that all?"

Indignation rode high. The crowd dispersed, muttering
at the injustice of life. Even Huldah, at Joanna's elbow,
snorted. "It's a pity that young Scot got no money for his
pains. He'd have done better to go after wolves. There's
twenty shillings paid for each of them that's killed."

Joanna sought out Ross. "What a sorry turn of events,"
she said.

"There's naught sorrowful," said Ross cheerily. " 'Tis a
great prize, this letter, one I'll treasure the rest of my days.
And Anoka found a reward that pleases him more than
any sum of gold." He put a hand on the shoulder of the
young Indian boy. "This is Pokanet," he said, "Anoka's
brother."

"His brother?" Joanna could hardly gasp out the words.

"Ye ken he'd been saving money to buy his mother
from slavery. He took it with him to Boston, and we
started to search for her. We finally found the man who
had captured her, one Jeremiah Grubb. He said she had
died, but that her son was living, sold to a weaver. We
went to nigh every weaver in Boston, I vow, and finally
found the lad. Did ye e'er see brothers more alike?"

Joanna studied the two dark faces, each aglow with
new-found knowledge. Was there something familiar
about the younger boy?

"Neither knew the other existed," continued Ross.
"Anoka's mother thought he'd been killed with the rest

of the family, and he'd no idea she was with child when she was captured."

Joanna looked again at Pokanet. Suddenly she saw him as he had been almost a year ago, standing on the wharf while Abner Leach haggled over his mother's purchase. Did the boy remember her? Was each detail of that fateful afternoon etched in his mind? Or had time, or the shock of the experience, mercifully wiped out the memory?

She could feel Ross's eyes upon her. They held a message of warning. In an instant she knew he was trying to tell her to say nothing. Anoka had enough bitter memories without one more added to his burden.

Anoka was shifting his feet restlessly, his eyes on the forest. "We go to my father," he said. "Anoka has much to teach a young brother of Indian ways." He moved away, the boy following him joyfully.

Once the excitement had died down, Joanna felt a wave of despair. For days she was so depressed she could scarcely do her work. She had been a fool to build such high hopes on the rumor of a reward. Why had she even listened to the talk?

The brief hope of freedom, however ill founded, had revived all her longing for liberty. She shrank from the weeks and months of servitude stretching before her. If only there were some way she could be loosed from the hateful yoke of indenture.

Dully she did her tasks. Soon they were finished. With Eliza Butt's help, she had time for sewing and mending. But Mistress Gifford had no needlework for her this day. What would she do? A phrase her mother had often used came to her mind. "Busy fingers best fight the megrims." Almost at once she knew what she'd do. She'd work at the loom. She bent to the weaving and soon found her old enthusiasm returning. The tartan was handsome. Ross would be pleased with it, she hoped.

She had been weaving for an hour or more when Dame Forrest hobbled into the room. In her gnarled hand she held a letter.

"You'd best hasten with the young Scot's plaid, my girl. There's little time left to finish it."

Joanna turned around in amazement. What was the meaning of this speech?

"I've had word from my brother in Devon," announced the dame. "His wife has died, God rest her soul, and he wants me to return to England to manage his household. A great estate he has, and servants needing a firm hand." Her tone was jubilant.

"Then you'll be leaving here," said Joanna. "I shall miss you." She could understand the older woman's joy. She had never been happy here in this new land under her daughter's roof.

"I've a surprise for you," continued Dame Forrest, her pale blue eyes twinkling. "You're to come with me, not as my maid, but as my companion. I'll pay your indenture and your passage to England as well. You can keep me cheered on the voyage and be my right hand in my brother's home. And in England we'll find a suitable match for you, my girl. You'll be able to dress as a lady once more. You can wear your satin gown and velvet cloak when we go aboard the ship."

Joanna put her hand on the loom and held fast to its

sturdy frame. Surely this was a fantasy, a dream from which she'd soon awaken.

The dry old voice went on. "We'll be leaving in a week or two. 'Twill be a tiresome voyage, but my last, I vow. Come now, are you not pleased?"

"Oh—oh, yes," stammered Joanna. She should be pleased. By rights she ought to be delirious with joy, half out of her mind with excitement. Here was all she'd been wishing for—release from servitude, escape from this Puritan land with its rigors and restrictions, and a suitable marriage. Was there a girl alive who didn't hope for such?

Yet all she could feel was a stunned surprise and a vague disappointment. Why was her heart as heavy as stone? Her spirits should be soaring. Instead she felt more depressed than ever. She would have to leave Hammersmith and all the friends she had made. She counted them over regretfully. There were the Whitings. Dear Mistress Whiting, what heart she had put into Joanna that winter night! And there was Maura, and all the Scots. They had befriended her warmly despite their own miserable state. And Yaweta. She had not seen the Indian girl since the night the pirates had been captured. How could she go away, not knowing what Yaweta's future would be?

Chiefly, there was Ross. She remembered him as he had started to pipe the lament for her father, then in the firelight when he had taught her to play the bagpipes. She could see him again struggling with Leach for the musket, and refusing later to be daunted by the lack of reward. How would he feel about her leaving? Would he rejoice that she had been freed? Or would he sink into lonely despair?

"Well, then, act as if you're pleased." The dame's voice cut across her thoughts. "You needn't come if you don't want to. I've no wish for an unwilling companion."

Joanna forced a smile and said, "I'm so surprised I scarce know what to say." She must have time to think. In two minutes she couldn't make a decision that would affect the rest of her lifetime.

All through the day she moved in a daze, hardly knowing whether her feet touched the ground or not. The Giffords made no mention of her change in fortune, but their attitude was eloquent. Debby clung to her and begged, "Will you make my poppet one more gown before you go?"

Huldah, grumbling over a kettle of stew, said, "I suppose you'll soon be preening your fine feathers, Miss Peacock!"

The news spread like wildfire. People stared at her in the street, their glances seeming to say, "Why should she have such good fortune?"

And Ross, meeting her as he left the casting shed, said generously, "I hear you'll be leaving us soon. I ken well 'tis happy ye'll be to get free from bondage."

"I'm not even sure that I'm going yet." What had made her say the words? Everyone seemed to take for granted that she would accept the dame's offer.

Ross's face brightened with a sudden light. "Ye might stay here, lass?" The naked hope in his eyes was almost too much. She could feel herself trembling.

"I don't know." She faltered. "I can't seem to make up my mind." It was true. She had thought of nothing else all day and all night, yet she could not come to a decision.

"I'd like it well were ye to stay," he said warmly. He

thought for a moment and added, "But 'tis your choice to make. There's no ither can make it for ye."

That evening Joanna knelt down in the bare garret beside her narrow bed. "May the Lord direct me in all my ways," she prayed. "May He guide me to do what is right." For long minutes she remained on her knees, seeking divine help. At last, refreshed and relieved, she lay down on her cot. The problem was in God's hands now. She would wait for an answer from Him. Soon she drifted into untroubled sleep.

When she awoke the next morning, the future was as clear as crystal. All her former indecision seemed unfounded. She would remain here in Hammersmith. Here were her friends, here was work she could do, here were people she could help. In England she had no family, no friends, nothing but bitter memories of a past that was forever gone—and an uncertain future. Here she had a useful present and the hope, at least, of happiness in the future. She had lived through nearly a year of indenture; she could endure three more. After that, she'd be free. After that. . . . The image of Ross floated into her mind, blocking out all other thoughts.

Telling Dame Forrest was the hardest of all. Her first disappointment soon turned to resentment. "I cannot understand you young people," she said. "Here I offer you everything, and you turn your back on me. I have never seen such ingratitude." She sank into a stormy silence.

Mistress Gifford took Joanna aside, suggested that she reconsider. Her uncle, Dame Forrest's brother, was a wealthy man. Joanna might have a rich future, should she find favor in his sight. He had sons of marriageable age, she confided.

The Iron Master seemed puzzled by her decision. And Huldah openly mocked her. "I thought ye'd some sense. Now I see ye've no more than Debby's poppet."

Only Mistress Whiting seemed to understand. She sought out Joanna after meeting and took her hands gently, looking deep into her eyes. "You have more vision than these others, my dear," she said. "You can see the possibilities of this new land. Would that there were more like you."

Joanna could feel her thoughts whirling. She'd made her decision and she would stick to it. But often doubt gnawed at her. Had she made the *right* decision?

22

The Iron Peacock

Doubtless Dame Forrest would take the loom back to Devon with her. In the few days left, Joanna worked frantically to finish the plaid for Ross. Soon it lay neatly folded on the old chest in the garret, and the loom stood empty and ready for dismantling and packing.

The day of Dame Forrest's departure arrived. Early in the morning she summoned Joanna to her chamber. It was the first time she had spoken directly to her since Joanna's decision not to accompany her to England.

"I'm leaving my loom for you," she said stonily. "I can no longer use it, and you're the only one here who has any interest in it. And that chest is for you. If you're determined to stay in this outport, you might as well have a few pretties to cheer you." She pointed to the carved oaken chest.

Joanna could feel tears starting to her eyes. In another minute she would be changing her mind, hastily preparing to accompany the older woman.

"Come here," commanded the dame. She pulled Joanna's head down to hers, gave her a stiff peck on the cheek. "Don't let that young Scot take you too far into the wilderness," she advised.

Joanna laid her smooth cheek against the parchment-like face. "Thank you," she said. "I'll take good care of your things, always."

"And take care of that young man, too," added Dame Forrest testily.

"But he's not even hinted at marriage," protested Joanna. She could feel the color blazing in her face.

"He will," said the older woman calmly, "in his own time." Then they were both caught up in the flurry of departure.

The Iron Master and his wife helped the dame aboard the shallop. Mistress Gifford would accompany her mother to Boston. They had been fortunate to find a young widow grateful to return to England as the dame's traveling companion. Mistress Gifford would have a chance to meet her and to see Dame Forrest safely aboard the ship.

Joanna and Debby stood on the wharf, waving at the shallop until it disappeared down the river's winding course. Hand in hand they climbed the hill.

Debby gave a skip of pleasure. "I'm glad you've not gone with Grandmamma. Now you can stay and play with me forever."

Forever? Joanna hoped the future would hold more than games with Debby.

Later that day Joanna took Debby to the Whitings'. She had not seen them to visit with since Yaweta had left, and in a way dreaded the meeting. The minister had been vastly distressed over Wapaket's death and Yaweta's return to her mother.

The Whiting family sat under the shade of a spreading maple. The minister was reading aloud from the Bible while the mother and daughters sat nearby, stringing beans. They greeted the newcomers joyfully.

Joanna sat down beside Mrs. Whiting, picked up a handful of the beans, and began to break the tips and pull off the strings. The younger girls jumped up and started a game of blindman's buff with Debby.

"Have you heard about Anoka's brother?" asked Joanna.

Yes, they had heard, the minister said. What had he done wrong, how had he failed, he asked, in his work with the Indians? "Ten years of working and praying, wiped out in a single day," he mourned. "How is it that John Eliot and others succeed in converting the savages where I cannot?"

"You did your best," said his wife comfortingly. "No man could do more."

They talked of other things, of Maura's and Duncan Muir's good fortune, and then Joanna rose to leave. She was about to go down the pathway to the road, when she saw three figures coming in single file from the riverbank. She rubbed her eyes in amazement, then cried out, "Yaweta is coming. And Anoka and his brother are with her."

The trio approached solemnly. Yaweta had never looked more graceful than in her deerskin dress with its trimming of brightly colored quills. Pokanet stood straight and slender in leather leggings and shirt. He looked more than ever like his brother. Anoka seemed older, invested with a new dignity and responsibility.

Yaweta set down a neat bundle of clothing beside

Mistress Whiting. "I came to bring back the dress and cloak you gave me," she said, "and to thank you for your care and friendship."

"You will always have our friendship," said Mistress Whiting, embracing her. "And you will always be welcome here."

"There is another reason why we have come," announced Yaweta. "We wish you to know that Anoka is now my husband, and that he has brought my mother to live with us. Both she and Pokanet now share our home. We want it to be a house like yours, where love and kindness rule."

Mistress Whiting's face glowed.

Joanna could not help recalling her visit to the Indian village with Yaweta during the winter. How far from love and kindness had been the hatred and selfishness she had seen there!

"Now I can truly honor my mother," continued Yaweta joyfully. Her face had lost its former troubled expression and bore a new contentment. She smiled shyly around the circle of eager faces.

Joanna threw her arms about the young Indian woman. "I hope you will be happy," she said, "and that you will still be my friend."

"We could never cease to be friends," said Yaweta. "Soon you and Mistress Whiting will come to visit our home. And Anoka wishes Mr. Whiting to come also and preach."

The minister raised his eyes to heaven. "And to think that moments ago I was filled with doubt," he said. "The seed has not fallen upon barren ground, but is flourishing."

Anoka lifted a warning hand. "Anoka not dress like

white man, not eat like white man," he said slowly. "Only learn about white man's God, good God, and powerful."

The minister nodded. He understands, thought Joanna. He knows that Anoka is trying to say he won't be like Wapaket. He'll keep to his own way of life, but he will accept some Christian beliefs. Perhaps, as time goes on, he will accept more and more.

Mr. Whiting took Anoka's hand solemnly. "I wish you well," he said. "May God bless your marriage and your plans for your people. I will gladly preach to them in your village."

Anoka shook the minister's hand ceremoniously. There was no doubt that this was a significant moment, full of promise.

Yaweta looked earnestly at Mr. Whiting. "It is good that you will come to teach our people. Anoka will be the sachem when his father dies. He may be able to lead the Indians to understand your God, and to keep peace between red men and white."

Anoka would make a good sachem, Joanna was certain. His own tragic experience had taught him the futility of war. She was sure he would persevere in his intent to keep peace.

For a few days Joanna and Huldah shared the responsibility of housekeeping and caring for Debby. Then Mistress Gifford returned from Boston, bubbling with energy and ideas. She had brought lengths of kersey and paduasoy and lustring for new gowns. She had even made sketches of the latest styles.

As Joanna studied the drawings, Mistress Gifford opened another parcel and drew forth two dress lengths of linen. The first was a mulberry color.

"I thought Huldah might like this," said the mistress diffidently.

Then she held up yards of blue-green linen. "And this is for you, Joanna. Does the peacock-blue please you? It should become your fair complexion and light hair."

Please her? After months of wearing the dull brown? Joanna could have sung with joy.

To her amazement, Mistress Gifford then suggested that Joanna move into Dame Forrest's bedchamber. It was light and airy, and would make an excellent sewing room. And Debby could move into the chamber over the porch. She was growing too old for the trundle bed in her parents' room. Debby was delighted. Now she could use the coverlet her grandmother had begun to weave and Joanna had finished.

Day after day Joanna cut and stitched and fitted. One gown she made for Mistress Gifford, a shimmering wine-colored paduasoy that set off her dark hair. Then a yellow frock for Debby and a tiny copy of it for her poppet. Now, said the mistress, Joanna must make her own.

But Joanna had seen the longing in Huldah's eyes. The poor thing had even less skill with the needle than the mistress, and she had need of a pretty gown. Putting her own aside, Joanna worked on Huldah's. Fitting Huldah was like covering a bolster, she thought. Where her waistline should be was a bulge. But at last the dress was ready. She would wear it to meeting on the Sabbath, said Huldah gleefully, smoothing the material over her ample bosom.

Now Joanna could cut into the blue-green cloth. She dared not make it in an elaborate style, knowing well the restrictions set by law. But she would put her best work into it. The material was excellent, a fine, well-woven linen. She could appreciate it the better for knowing something about weaving now.

She'd make the bodice pointed and laced down the front with ribbons. She'd make the neckline square, the sleeves to just below the elbow. And on the skirt she'd set rows of tucks to give the cloth more body and make it stand out more. There was a bit of fine white linen left over from a pinafore of Debby's. She could use that for a falling band a hand's breadth wide around the neckline.

Late one afternoon Joanna took the last stitch in her gown, and went downstairs to help with supper, which was to be early. The mistress had a headache and wished to retire as soon as the meal was over. Mr. Gifford had an evening appointment with the magistrate.

When the meal had been cleared away, Joanna hurried upstairs to her bedchamber. Each time she stepped inside the door she gave the room a silent greeting. She could imagine the loom and chest welcoming her in turn. How wonderful to have so pleasing a chamber after months in the shadowy garret!

Hastily she stripped off her brown skirt and bodice. She washed her face and combed her hair. Then she slipped the blue-green gown over her head, laced up the bodice, and adjusted the soft ruffle of the falling band.

She put her hands on her slim waist. The dress fitted well, she knew. There was a small wavy mirror in the corner. She peered into it but could see only a hint of blue in the glass.

What should she do now? She looked about the room. She supposed she should change back into her old dress. There was no reason in the world for her to keep this one on, now that she knew the fit was right.

Her eyes lighted on the carved oaken chest. She'd glanced hastily at its contents the day Dame Forrest left, but Debby had drawn her away before she'd finished. She had seen many of the things before when she had helped the dame rearrange them. But she had been too occupied with dressmaking recently to look them over thoroughly. She might as well do it now while there was yet light to see by. If only there was a tippet or a shawl to go with her new dress!

She lifted the heavy lid, propped it open, and knelt down before the chest. Here was a coverlet woven by the dame, like the one Joanna had finished. Here were linen towels, bed sheets, and bolster slips. There was a quilted green satin petticoat. When would she ever have a chance to wear that? And here, in one corner, was a small silk bag covered with embroidery. She'd not seen that before. What could it contain? She took it in her hands. It was heavy. With mounting excitement she untied the strings and upended the bag. Gold coins fell into the chest, and with them a folded square of paper. Trembling, she opened it and read:

Dear Joanna:

This is the sum I would have spent for your passage to England. I leave it for you to use as you wish. Enjoy it with my blessing.

Faithfully,
Enid Forrest

How long she knelt there, Joanna could not tell. The sunshine had faded into twilight's dimness, and the first stars were shining in the sky when she carefully replaced the coins in the bag and tucked it back in the corner of the chest.

For the time being she would tell no one about Dame Forrest's gift. For a little while she would keep the knowledge to herself. It was too precious to share as yet. But one day, when the time was right, she would tell the Giffords and pay off her indenture. If they were willing, she would remain with them, doing the sewing and mending and perhaps some weaving. They would want to make some payment to her, she supposed, as they did to Huldah.

She rose to her feet and stretched her arms wide. Here she was, in the same room, under the same roof as before, yet how different everything seemed! Although she was still a bond servant, she now had the means to be free, to leave at any time she wished. And the strangest part of all was that for the present this was where she wanted to remain.

The ratatat of the iron knocker on the front door broke in upon her thoughts. There was a pause; then it sounded again. Why did Huldah not go to the door? Then she recalled that Huldah had gone to visit Goody Talbot, taking Debby with her. She hurried down the stairs, swung the heavy door wide, and stepped back in surprise.

Ross stood just outside. Instead of his usual leathern doublet and woolen breeches, he wore kilt and plaid. He regarded her with equal astonishment.

"Ye've a new gown," he said admiringly, "in a color I like right well to see on ye."

She was so flustered she had almost forgotten her manners. "Will you come in?" she invited.

Huldah had left a Betty lamp burning. By its light Joanna could see how threadbare his plaid was.

"I've come to see the Iron Master," said Ross, "on a

matter of import. But first I'd like a word with ye, if ye've time."

She had all the time in the world. She ushered him into the keeping room. "Mr. Gifford has gone out," she explained, "though he may soon return."

"That will give me a chance to talk with ye, then," he said soberly. He sat on a wainscot chair, she on the settle, spreading her new skirt wide.

"Ye've heard of Duncan's good fortune?" he asked. She nodded.

"Duncan's already bought his freedom," he said, "and now he insists on paying off my indenture as well. At first I wouldna hear of it, but he's that set on it I was convinced at last. 'Tis understood I'll pay back every farthing." A broad smile lightened his face.

"There's no one deserves good fortune more than you," she said firmly. She could rejoice wholeheartedly for him.

Then fear struck at her. "Will you be going back to Scotland?" she asked. Of course that was where he would go. Ever since she'd known him he'd been longing to return to the heather and the highlands, to the life he'd left for battle.

"I have thought of it," he said. "For months 'twas all I could dream of. But of late I've come to realize that, with my father dead and the laird gone, there's no one to draw me back. My mother died when I was a wee lad, and I've nae living kin to call my ain."

Joanna sighed deeply, partly in sympathy, partly in relief. "I feel so about England."

"But that's only part of it," Ross went on. "I keep thinking about this New World we dwell in. Men have got but a foothold in it now. There are miles of it no white man has ever seen. 'Tis a new land, and some of it is free for the taking. I'd like well to stay here and make my mark upon it."

He was going to stay. Joanna could feel her heart pounding and the blood drumming in her ears. Ross was not going to Scotland. He was going to remain here in the Bay Colony.

"Will you be going far off?" she asked. "Perhaps to a new settlement with Duncan?"

"Not yet," he answered. "I could go with him, were I so minded. But I'm just beginning to get some knowledge of the Iron Works. It must be hard for a woman to understand how a man can get wrought up over furnaces and hammers and slitting mills. Ye ken the works fair fascinate me. I'll not be satisfied till I've mastered every process."

"So you'll stay at Hammersmith?"

"For a while, at least. Then I might venture out on my own and set up a small plant some distance away, where men will be needing tools and implements."

"And kettles," she added, "and firebacks."

He gave her a quizzical glance from his dark eyes. "I brought something with me to show ye. I left it outside. 'Twill take but a minute to fetch it."

She had something to show him, too. Swiftly she ran up the stairs, picked up the tartan. She was coming down the staircase, the woolen folds over her arm, when Ross came in the door. He looked first at the plaid she was carrying, then at the plaid over his shoulder.

"And what have ye there?" he asked, his brow wrinkling.

" 'Tis something I wove on the loom for you," she said.

"The colors may not be exactly true, but they were the nearest I could get." She held the tartan out to him.

He laid a large flat parcel down on the table and took the tartan. He unfastened the old, worn plaid from his shoulder and put it on a bench. Then he shook out the new material, folded it, and draped it in the same fashion as the old. Tilting his head to one side, he inspected the plaid critically.

"As fine as e'er was loomed in Scotland," he said largely. Then he held out a corner and squinted at it, thrusting out his lower lip.

"Is this the whole of what ye wove?"

"Yes." What could be wrong?

"There's not e'en a wee bit more?"

"No."

"It's too bad to put ye to the trouble, but ye must weave some more."

"More?" She couldn't understand. "That is exactly the same length as your old plaid. I measured it carefully."

" 'Tis the right length for this, all right, but there'll be need for enough more for a woman's shawl. Know ye not that the women of the clan wear a shawl of the McCrae tartan?"

She could only stand there while blushes suffused her cheeks.

"I canna ask ye what I have in mind until I speak to Mr. Gifford for your hand. But ye might want to look at this whilst we're waiting."

He fumbled with the wrappings of the parcel and drew out a flat piece of white pine, rectangular in shape.

" 'Tis the mold for the fireback I was telling ye about.

I'd like well to cast it soon, so that when I build a house I can set it in the chimney back."

He laid the mold on the table and held the lamp so that light shone on the carving. Taking up the central space, its delicate head lifted high, its magnificent tail feathers spread in a wide fan, was a peacock. In the upper left-hand corner was the letter *J*, opposite it *R*, and beneath the peacock's feet *McC*.

Joanna stared at it, speechless. All these months while she had hardly dared to dream, Ross had been working and planning for this moment.

"'Tis the way I first saw ye, as pretty as a peacock in your velvet cloak, with your head held high. I thought then ye were as proud as one, but I've learned different since. 'Tis not pride, but courage ye have, lass. Ye've the strength of iron."

She gazed at him, her heart in her eyes. Then the Iron Master's step sounded in the hallway. Ross gave her a long look.

"Ye're willing that I should speak to him?"

"Oh, yes," she breathed.

"I'll be back," he said, and went to meet Mr. Gifford.

Joanna waited, her heart singing, tracing the design of the peacock with her finger. The strength of iron, Ross had said. It would not be easy to live up to his expectations. But she would try. She would keep on trying for the rest of her days.

Author's Note

Every thread in this book's fabric is spun from the stuff of which history is made, although fact and fancy have been freely interwoven in the telling of the story.

All the background is authentic—the Iron Works, the blockhouse, Puritan customs, indenture, Indian slavery, and the selling of the Scottish prisoners into seven years' service to the Iron Master.

Most of the characters are fictitious, but based upon individuals who helped to settle New England. Mr. Gifford and Mr. Whiting, both of whom left an indelible mark upon local history, are depicted from clues gleaned from existing records. All other people in the story are imaginary, although representative of the courageous souls who dreamed and despaired and faced countless perils in this foothold on the edge of a new continent.

Readers who like to see the locale of a story may wish to visit the Ironworks Restoration in Saugus, Massachusetts, including the Iron Master's house and, about one mile distant, the house reputed to have been the dwelling of the Scots captured at Dunbar and indentured to the Iron Master.

MARY STETSON CLARKE lives in Melrose, Massachusetts, north of Boston and near Saugus, the setting for her second novel, *The Iron Peacock*. Perhaps because her forebears were among the first settlers to come to New England, she feels strongly that their early struggles for freedom of thought and action should not be forgotten, or lightly accepted.

Mrs. Clarke was educated in Melrose public schools, majored in English at Boston University, and studied writing as a graduate student at Columbia University. In her girlhood she was encouraged to write by her parents and brothers. Her husband and three children have continued that encouragement. She balances her interest in the past by taking an active part in community affairs.

Exploring historically rich areas has a perennial fascination for her, and she confesses that she cannot pass by a venerable house, a mossy stone wall, or a weed-choked lane without wishing that she could reconstruct their stories. When she visited the restoration of the Saugus Ironworks, she felt a strong compulsion to write a tale about the dauntless men and women whose labors made it one of the wonders of the New World.